Lock Down Publications and Ca$h
Presents

CORNER
BOY
CHRONICLES 2
BURY ME A BOSS

Written By
COREY ROBINSON

First Edition 2025

Printed in the United States of America

This is a work of fiction. Names, characters, places, and incidents either are products of the author's imagination or are used fictitiously. Any similarity to actual events or locales or persons, living or dead, is entirely coincidental.

Lock Down Publications
P.O. Box 944
Stockbridge, GA 30281
www.lockdownpublications.com

Like our page on Facebook: Lock Down Publications
www.facebook.com/lockdownpublications.ldp

Stay Connected with Us!

Text **LOCKDOWN** to 22828 to stay up-to-date with new releases, sneak peaks, contests and more…

Like our page on Facebook:
Lock Down Publications

Join Lock Down Publications/The New Era Reading Group

Visit our website:
www.lockdownpublications.com

Follow us on Instagram:
Lock Down Publications

Email Us: We want to hear from you!

Note From the Author

What's up, Homestead! Shout out to all my people—Milly, Joy, Toye, Tyra and Smurf, Miss Glo, Amber Leah, Pauline, Kizzy, Carrie Jones, and one to never be forgotten, Pate.

Believe in yourself, and you can achieve anything. There are no limits to how high you can climb, but you have to be willing to get on the ladder.

Don't forget to like me on `Facebook` @coreyRobinson (Author).

Chapter 1

Jamir felt the pressure on the head of his dick and struggled to open his eyes. He was still a little woozy. His vision was blurred, so it took him a second to focus on what was happening. When Jamir was finally able to look down, he could only see a female's head. Her hand was wrapped around the base of his manhood, and when he realized who it was, he shoved her off his semi-erect manhood. He struggled to pull himself onto the bed and heard the female start to giggle. Jamir was angry because he didn't see anything funny about the situation.

"The fuck? What's so damn funny, Tomeka? What the hell is you doin', slobin' on my dick? Do Raw know you in here? Because, bitch, I don't play them type of fuck games! Somebody needs to enlighten me on what the hell is goin' on."

Tomeka smacked her pouty lips. "You don't need to worry about Raw anymore, because she ain't in no position to know a damned thing, because her no-good, big, black, wanna-be-a-man ass is six feet under the dirt. Danny made sure of that."

Jamir, still a little dazed, began to think back on the last events that took place, and the last thing he could remember was Raw was standing over him, injecting his arm with something. Meanwhile, Danny stood nearby, holding a gun in front of him. Jamir was confused as to why Tomeka said Danny made sure Raw was in the dirt. Jamir could have sworn the two of them had been working together to eliminate him. He began to wonder where they were and how he'd ended up naked, with Tomeka giving him head. This was Raw's main bitch.

The confusion dazed him, but he was determined to remember what had happened. He scrunched his eyebrows and looked around the room. He didn't recognize the pink and gray butterfly-print curtains or the seventy-inch flat-screen TV mounted on the wall. Jamir couldn't recognize anything except the bitch in front of him.

He quickly jumped up and began searching for his clothes. Jamir couldn't remember the exact clothes he'd been wearing. All he knew was he had to find them, and he would know them once he saw them. He began to feel overwhelmed, so he stood up and placed his hand on his forehead.

"What the fuck?"

He needed a moment to regain his senses and for the room to stop spinning so he could take a moment to look for each article of his clothing. After the room began to seemingly stop spinning, he sat back down on the bed quietly.

Once he got his mental state to handle all of what he remembered, he said, "Oh, shit! This dyke ass bitch dosed me with heroin! That's what the fuck was in that needle! What the hell I'ma do?"

Tomeka eased herself beside him to calm him down. "No, Jamir. She thought it was heroin. In fact, it was only crushed sleeping pills. I found where she had the syringes stashed, and while she was out on the block, I switched them. The dumb bitch ain't even have a clue that I knew what she was up to. I overheard her on the phone, wit' her snake ass, plotting with some nigga named Malcolm. They came up with a plan to take you out of the game. There was no way I was gonna let that happen. That was real foul and fucked up on her part because, if my memory serves me correctly, you were the reason she even made it to where she did in the game. And that, for me, was low-down. I can't stand a greedy, back-stabbing bitch, even if she did belong to me. If she could do it to you, what about me? Was I next on her list?"

Jamir could believe what Tomeka was saying. Raw was talkin' to some nigga named Malcolm, plotting on him, but the only Malcolm Jamir knew was his connect.

"Meka, are you sure you heard her right? She was on the phone with a nigga name Malcolm? That can't be right, 'cause it seems to me Danny and Raw were the ones that teamed up against me to take me out, not someone else."

"Um, yes, I'm sure, Jamir, I know what the hell I heard. Besides, Danny was on your side and still is. When I heard that phone conversation, I went to Danny and told him what was about to go down. Together, we came up with a plan to switch the heroin in the syringe to the sleeping pills. He continued to talk shit about you with Raw, only to get her to think he wanted you out of the game in hopes she would include him in whatever her plan was. But she was too greedy and dumb to suspect a thing. If you ask me, the bitch got what she deserved. My momma always told me to never bite the hands that feed you. I have tried to live by those words my entire life. Raw didn't appreciate all that you did for her. But a bitch like me would never take you for granted."

"That's nice to know and all, but can you please explain to me how I ended up naked in a strange bed with yo' lips wrapped around my dick."

"Shit, I seen an opportunity and decided this was my chance to see what that dick do. I have never been the type of bitch to let a good moment pass me by. You might as well let me go ahead and finish."

"Nice try, but that ain't gon' happen. I don't fuck behind muthafuckas I done partnered with, even if they do me dirty. That's an unwritten rule. I'm a thorough nigga, and I stick by being a real one."

7

"Ok, cool. That's yo' loss. Can't blame a bitch for trying though, 'cause my head game is top tier, and this pussy stays wet and ready."

Tomeka slowly lay back and then ran her fingers over her lips. Then she spread her legs to give him what she claimed to be truth—her wet pussy.

Jamir smirked and shook his head at her boldness. She was cute, especially when she exposed her plump clit, hardened and ready. For a quick second, he started to reconsider, but with his loyalty to the code, he wasn't willing to compromise. He also knew that his sex game was known to cause havoc, so he didn't want to put that in her life, considering what she'd done for him. He didn't want her to end up being another headache he didn't need or want.

Resisting the urge, he said, "That's why you should give it to somebody that need it because I'm straight on some pussy. Now, can you please tell me where my clothes at? I need to get the hell outta here. I got some questions I need answered."

"Fine, Jamir. They're still in the laundry room. I washed them so that they would be nice and clean for you. Ohh, and don't get mad when you see me on the next hustler's arm. You had your chance." Tomeka got off the bed and walked out of the room without saying another word. She was pissed. Jamir looked up just in the time to see her ass cheeks jiggle with every step she took.

She wasn't too happy with being rejected by him. She made sure to walk with a purpose. She wanted him to see what he had passed up on. Jamir could feel his dick thump a little at the sight of her, but he knew there wasn't shit he could do about it.

Tomeka's curves went on for days, and any other nigga in the hood would have jumped on that opportunity to ride them, but Jamir just couldn't bring himself to do it. He already had enough drama going on in his life with having to deal with Erica, who he was stuck dealing with for eighteen long ass years, was still mad at himself for slipping up and getting her pregnant. Although he loved his daughter, he wished he could somehow take back the night he went up in Erica raw.

Jamir hadn't been ready to be a father. He felt he was still too young, but what was done was done. He would talk trash to Danny about how Danny had slipped, yet Jamir had turned around and done the same thing. Jamir had plans for his life that he couldn't pursue anymore because he now had responsibilities. He refused to be a deadbeat dad like his father. He vowed he would always be there for his shorty.

Jamir looked down at his watch, the only thing of his that he had on at this point. He then realized that it was taking Tomeka a long time to come back with his clothes. After the events that had taken place, he hoped she wasn't pulling a snake move. She didn't seem like the type. After his rejection, though, he was unsure. In fact, he was confused about plenty of things. Jamir thought a man couldn't put anything past a female, especially one who was in her feelings. A bitch would turn from saint to sinner in the blink of an eye when things didn't go their way, and after what happened, he most definitely wasn't about to get caught slipping again.

Now a little more focused, Jamir scanned the room and stood to look around the unfamiliar room again. At a glance, he noticed an ajar door between two dressers. He wondered for a second why he hadn't noticed it before. Feeling the urge to use the toilet, Jamir hoped the door would lead him to a bathroom before he pissed himself.

Jamir walked over toward the door then slowly turned the knob. He didn't know what would be on the other side. He wished he had his gun on him in times like this. Looking around the room again, he was sure it was nowhere to be found.

"Shit!" He mumbled as he remembered he'd left it in his car when he went to Raw's house. He trusted her and didn't feel the need to have it. If he had known what was bound to happen, he would surely have had it on his right hip and blasted Raw and anybody else who wanted to take him out. He promised himself he would never — as long as there was breath in his body —.make that mistake again.

Jamir opened the door and breathed a sigh of relief when he noticed it was indeed a bathroom. He rushed ahead, right to the toilet. He felt like he had been pissing for an hour as he emptied every ounce of fluid he had. Once he sensed the last drop, he immediately went to the sink to wash his hands. Naked as could be, Jamir started to look around the tiny bathroom to see if there was anything he could use to cover himself up—a towel, a robe, something. He spotted a pink, furry robe hanging on the wall but thought to himself that he would die before he put that shit on. Then he saw a bath towel on the door and grabbed it to wrap it around his waist.

Jamir walked out the bathroom, determined to find out what was taking Tomeka so long to come back with his clothes. Before he could take another step, he heard a male's voice coming from the other side of the door. Jamir leaned in closer to see if he could recognize who the voice belonged to, and once he recognized the male's voice, he stepped out the door and stood on the other side, listening to the conversation that Danny and Tomeka were having. When he realized that they weren't talkin' about shit, he stepped all the way into the living room where they were having their conversation.

Jamir saw Tomeka and Danny in each other's arms. Jamir was a little confused because Tomeka had just left the bedroom, ready to wet his dick up with her juicy box. Jamir had already deemed her a hoe, but for this, she was out of hand.

"Aye, the fuck is going on in here? Girl, you a wild one. How you in here with the next man when you was just in there trying to ride my dick? Type of fuck games is you playing? Where the hell is my clothes?"

Tomeka pulled back from Danny and turned to Jamir. With anger, she placed one hand on her hip then sucked her teeth. She fiercely walked over to the couch where she had Jamir's clothes lying out. She picked them up and threw them at him.

"First of all, there your damned clothes. Go. And I don't have to explain shit to you. I'm a grown, single-ass woman. This my pussy, and I can do with it whatever I please. You got a bitch begging you for the dick, but nigga, there are plenty more dudes out here that would love to have an ass like mine all up on them. What? You thought I was gonna be sitting in the corner, crying and shit? No, I don't think so. I don't get down like that. On to the next one." Tomeka didn't feel like she had to explain anything to Jamir. But because she was what she deemed to be a strong, bad bitch, she had to let him know. What one man didn't want, three or more did.

Tomeka looked at Jamir then at Danny and rolled her eyes at both. Then she walked out of the room. Tomeka's ego had already been bruised by Jamir when he turned her down. There was no way he was gonna do it twice in the same night. Tomeka felt she had top-tier pussy, and any man would jump at the chance to lay pipe down in it, but Jamir was one of one, but there was no way she was gonna allow his rejection to knock her off her throne. It was his loss, she felt.

Jamir began to put on his clothes, and once he felt Tomeka was out of range to hear what he and Danny were about to talk about, Jamir was ready to get down to the bottom of this. He wanted some answers.

"So, D? Nigga, the fuck you was doing in cahoots with Raw? I thought you hated that bitch for stealing some pussy you was fucking. When the hell did you and her become friends?"

"Come on, Jamir. You and I both know that if I was in cahoots with that bitch, your ass would be six feet under."

"Then why you ain't put me up on game as soon as you found out what she was up to? That shit should have never been played that far."

"I ain't tell your ass, 'cause you would have thought I was only saying that to throw salt on her name to get her out of the picture. I told you from the jump that dyke was no good, but I needed you to see it for yourself. You never would have believed me if you hadn't. I had to go along with the plan to show you. But you good, bro. I had your back."

"Yeah, you did, but you damned sure had me fooled for a minute. Thanks for looking out, though."

"Anytime, every time, Jamir. We go too far back to let a snake muthafucka slither in between us. But you do know Raw wasn't your only problem. The real issue is that fuck nigga Malcolm. That's who needs to be handled."

"Yeah. That's what Meka said. But I'm having a real hard time believing that shit, man. She had to have had a misunderstanding because I ain't never known Malcolm to be a disloyal type of nigga. I have been dealing with him for a long time. And other than that shit with Rachel, we ain't never had no issues."

"Ohh, you talking about that white bitch that you got a thing for? That shit crazy, but now that you mentioned it, how you know all that shit wasn't a set up on her behalf? I mean, come on now, Jamir. Can you really ever trust a crackhead? Muthafuckas will do anything for that shit, even turn on your ass."

Jamir got quiet and thought about what Danny had said, and even though he knew his boy was right, he didn't want to feed him bullshit. It was a proven fact that dope fiends would turn on their own family just for a piece of that rock. Jamir, however, refused to believe that Rachel would do anything to put him in harm's way. Had she known Malcolm was his people, she never would have fucked with him. But the real question was, did Malcolm know who she was? Jamir knew that was something he needed to find out.

"Ya know, D? I'm with you when you are right. Them smokers will do anything, even sell they own soul if they could, just for that shit. But Rachel? Rachel ain't that type of broad. You can't classify her in the same category as those other fiends out there. She's just different."

"Damn, nigga. That hoe must got some bomb ass pussy or something `cause that shit got your mind messed up. You talking crazy as a muthafucka, but you can say what you want. That bitch ain't no different from anyone of them muthafuckas that get high. As long as she suckin' on that glass dick, she ain't no different from the rest. Come on, man. We all know, once they become a crackhead, they ass will always be a crackhead."

Danny shook his head and leaned on the chair. He reached into his pocket, where he had a bottle of Percocet, and pulled it out. He opened the bottle and shook a couple of pills into the palm of his hand, then reached over to offer Jamir one, which he refused. Pills just weren't his thing. Plus, he could still feel the effects of the sleeping pills that had been injected into his veins. He couldn't handle anything else in his system.

Danny ended up throwing up both pill bottles in his mouth, and no sooner than he swallowed them, Tomeka walked into the room, butt-ass naked.

Danny licked his lips and grabbed a firm hold on his dick. The Percs would take a little while to kick in, but Tomeka instantly had him on cloud nine. If Danny wouldn't have had pants on, his shit would have shot straight up because Tomeka had him on swole.

Jamir looked from Danny to Tomeka and walked out, leaving them to do whatever they wanted. He wasn't about to be a witness to anything, because he was still trying to figure out what the hell was going on.

Once he got outside, he stood still for a minute, contemplating his next move. He scanned the parking lot for a car he recognized but saw nothing. He thought about going back inside to question Tomeka and Danny about where his ride was but decided against it. Instead, he pulled his hoodie over his head and put one foot in front of the other. Jamir checked his pockets but found them empty, so he shrugged his shoulders and kept it moving.

Jamir walked and thought about all the shit he had been through. All he ever wanted to do was to rise in the game and be a boss. But it seemed every time he turned around, another obstacle stood in his way.

However, he refused to give up on what he wanted. He had already put in more work, and Jamir had never been a quitter. He may never make it to the Pablo Escobar status, but he would push as hard as he could to get there. Or even come close to it.

Jamir paid close attention to everything and everyone. As he walked home, he couldn't be sure about who his enemies were, so he played it cautiously. Everyone around him was now a suspect. He hated to live like that, but he no longer had a choice. It seemed like those he trusted couldn't be trusted at all.

It had grown dark by the time Jamir turned onto his street. He'd been walking for what seemed like hours, and all he wanted to do was relax and rest. When Jamir got closer to his house, he could see his car parked out front and wondered who had brought it there.

He opened his car door and immediately reached under the driver's seat. Thankfully, his weapon was still there, right where he left it. He then checked the middle console and found his wallet and his money. He was shocked that not one dollar was missing because he thought he would have been robbed after all that had taken place. He was grateful that he hadn't.

Jamir grabbed his things, and just as he was about to close the door, he saw movement from the corner of his eye. He dropped everything but his weapon and pointed it toward the back seat of his ride. Sweat beads formed on his brow because he had no clue of what to expect, but when he saw Rachel's big, green eyes looking back at him, he breathed a sigh of relief.

She had always brought him peace in troubled times, so he was glad to see her. However, he remembered the last time they were together, things hadn't gone too well, because she had already found out about his daughter. He hoped they could see eye to eye about it because his daughter would always be a part of his life.

"Rachel? The fuck is you doin' in my back seat?"

Jamir could tell that Rachel was high, and it pissed him off instantly. The thought of her smoking that shit in his ride made him want to snatch her out of it, but the last thing he needed was a case for beating a bitch's ass, especially a white one.

"Where have you been, Jamir? With her and your kid? I have come by here every night for eight days straight, and you haven't been here at all. Last night, I was just so tired of going back and forth, so I decided to get in the back seat and wait for you. I guess I must have fallen asleep, but here you are."

"Wait. You said eight days? You sure about that?"

"Yes, I'm sure. The last time we were together, you told me about your daughter with that bitch, and it really upset me, so I left without telling you how I felt. I wanted to come back and let you know, but you were gone without a trace, and I haven't seen you since. I even checked on the block, but nothing."

"Come on, Rach. Follow me inside. I got some shit I want to discuss with you."

Jamir held the seat up so Rachel could get out of his ride. Once she stepped out, he checked the back to make sure she didn't leave anything behind that could later get him cased up. When he saw that all was clear, he shut the door, but not before he locked it. The last thing he needed was someone else taking up camp in his ride. He would have cursed Rachel out, but he was going to need her, so he decided against it.

As soon as Rachel walked into his house, she sat on the couch and leaned back. She was exhausted because she hadn't had any real rest in days. When Jamir told her that he had a daughter, it broke her heart, so she used that as an excuse to go out and get high. As soon as she took the first hit, she felt guilty, but not guilty enough to stop.

Rachel had been smoking crack nonstop for days and hadn't even eaten anything. Her stomach hurt from the hunger pains, but she ignored it. However, as soon as Jamir heard her stomach growl, he said something.

"Fuck is the last time you ate? Your shit angrier than a muthafucka, growling and shit. Get yo' ass up and get something to eat from the fridge."

"I'm not hungry. And don't worry about my stomach. You wasn't worried about it when you got that bitch pregnant."

"Oh, so we still on that? Why don't you take yo' petty ass on in the bathroom and wash up so you can get on something else—like this dick—unless, of course, you already dicked out for the night."

"You know what, Jamir? Fuck you and your dick. You turning out to be just like every other nigga anyway. You care about you and only you! You don't give a damn about me or my feelings. You say what you think I wanna hear just to get some pussy, but you don't mean any of it."

"Oh, yeah? Well, since you think I'm like every other nigga out there, that means I ain't gotta say shit to get that pussy. All I have to do is pull out some of that package of dope and dangle it in your face, and yo' fuckin' panties and knees will drop to the floor. With yo' worn, cracked-out ass. The nerve of me to think that I could parade you around in my shit like you was my lady, but, bitch, you don't belong to me. You belong to the streets. Now, you and all yo' attitude can get the fuck up out my shit, and fast."

16

The words Jamir Spoke hit Rachel in the chest like a ton of bricks. People talked shit to her all the time, but only Jamir's words had the power to hurt her, and he knew it. Rachel stood and did all she could to hold back her tears. She was going to do just what he told her. Leave.

She walked slowly to the door because her heart was so heavy that she couldn't move any faster. Rachel put her hand on the knob but turned to look at Jamir once more. She swore in her mind that she was done with him, but he proved her wrong.

"Wait. Don't leave. I need to holler at you about something first."

Rachel lowered her hand from the knob and stepped away from the door. He had been all she'd ever wanted, and she hated that. It made her weak to his demands. Rachel damned herself for being such a fool, but the hold he had on her couldn't be a broken one.

Rachel walked back to the couch, sitting down in the same seat she'd been in before. She took a deep breath, as if she were about to go underwater, and with a defeated expression, she looked at Jamir.

"What is it you want, Jamir? I don't stay where I'm not welcome. Go ahead. Speak your piece so I can, in your words `get the hell up outta yo' shit and fast'. Isn't that what you just said to me, Jamir?"

"I need to know. That night you was held up in the room with my connect—Malcolm—did you help set me up to get me outta of the game? Was that the reason you was with him?"

Rachel scrunched her eyebrows together because she was a little put off by the question. He had caught her completely off guard. She knew that Jamir could see the confusion in her face. Rachel thought about what he had just asked her for a moment. A few minutes before she responded, because she honestly wasn't even sure how to answer him, she gathered her words and then gave them to him raw and uncut.

"Are you implying that I knowingly hooked up with him just to plan a setup on you? Wow. Jamir, I can't believe a thought like that would even enter your mind. However, it has made me realize that you really think so little of me. It's ok, though. I'm a big girl, and I don't need your validation or anything else. Yes, I may smoke crack, suck a little dick here and there, and even fuck niggas that I just met, but one thing I'm not is a snake. How dare you even disrespect my character by thinking I would do something so disloyal, especially to you. I don't need this bullshit in my life, Jamir. I'm just sorry it took me this long to realize that."

Rachel stood from the couch once again and rushed to the door. Jamir knew just how to strike a nerve in her, but she had grown tired of the back and forth. One minute, he wanted her, and the next, he pushed her away. She just couldn't take it anymore. She yanked the front door open and started to walk out. But once again, Jamir had something to say.

"Look. Rachel, please don't leave. I'm sorry for that crazy shit, alright?"

Rachel turned to him and looked into his eyes. She wasted so much time trying to please him and live up to his standards, but she finally realized that he didn't have any. She was truly done with him, and no amount of sorry was going to change that.

"You know what, Jamir? You don't need to be sorry; you need to be careful. Open your eyes and see who it really is that's a snake in your life. When you ride with the devil, you start growing horns, and the tips of yours is already showing. I'm sure that it was your partner who put those thoughts about me in your head, but instead of me, it should be him you question, especially ones about your sister. Goodbye, Jamir, and forget you ever knew me."

Rachel walked out and slammed the door behind her, leaving Jamir with a lot to think about. The mention of his sister brought back raw feelings for him and put his emotions on high. She had been dead and gone for a while, but Jamire still wondered about how she died. If he found out Danny had anything to do with it, he was going to pay. First, he had to find out what was going on with Malcolm. The only problem was the person he needed to help him had just walked out the door.

Chapter 2

"That's right, Tomeka. You suckin' the hell out this dick. Ah, shit, a nigga about to bust all in yo' mouth"

Tomeka stopped and looked at Danny, frowning in disgust. She had only been down there for a couple of minutes. She knew her head game was fire but couldn't believe he was already moaning that he was about to cum. This was a record for her. Never, ever had she been able to make a man cum in under two minutes.

Danny had to have been trippin'. He messed her whole mood up, and she wasn't happy about it. She let go of his swollen dick and gave him a piece of her mind.

"Hold the fuck up, nigga. I know damn well you ain't about to tap out on me like that? Oh, hell no. I ain't even been on it for a good two minutes, and you ready to blow. Didn't you say that the Perc keep you up longer? What the hell is up with that? I was trying to get freaky as hell with you. What type of bullshit is this?" Tomeka was mad and horny, ready to pop her pussy all on his dick. A hard dick, not some soft, limp noodle.

"You know what? Yo' ass is ghetto as fuck, but because of yo' mouth game, I'ma overlook that shit. Damn, I wouldn't be bustin' so fast if yo' lips wasn't so soft and the way you took all of this pipe down yo' throat. That shit felt like you swallowed it whole. Give me a quick minute. Let me get back right, and when I do, I'ma knock the lining out that pussy."

"What the hell ever, Danny. You talk a real good game, but from what I see, you for damn sure can't back it up. I don't have time to be wasting like this."

Tomeka had always wanted to be a baller's wife, and when she hooked up with Raw, she thought she hit the jackpot. By the time she realized Raw was just a small fish in a big pond, she was stuck, not because she wanted to stay, but because Raw wouldn't allow her to leave.

Raw felt like she owned Tomeka, and there was no leaving her. Tomeka was Raw's arm candy. She was only on her arm for show. Raw really hadn't given a damn about her for a while now, and there was no way that she was going to allow anyone else to ever possess her like that. For a long time, Tomeka was very unhappy and fed up, which was one of the reasons she helped Jamir and Danny end Raw's hold on her. The only person she wanted to hook up with was Jamir, but he couldn't care less about how beautiful she was or how wet the pussy got. He didn't want her.

In her mind, she hoped messing with Danny would make Jamir see her in a different light and change his mind about her. She would have to settle to try and find out what Danny was up to so that Jamir would be thankful and reward her for the way she felt he should have already been feeling.

She never thought of him as an ungrateful bastard, but he damned sure acted like one. After all, she was the one who saved him from being turned into a heroin addict. Tomeka thought back to the phone conversation she had overheard. She remembered everything said as if she had just heard it. She wondered why everyone seemed to want to push Jamir out of the way so badly. It wasn't like he was really big in his status, nor did he push much dope. At least she didn't think so. Tomeka thought Jamir was good people, and even though he had dissed her, she would still play along with Danny until she could figure out his whole game plan.

Tomeka watched as Danny lay on the couch and stroked his dick in hopes of getting it back up. She was a freak and wanted to fuck, but with Danny, she would have to get her pleasure in increments. He couldn't even stay up long enough to keep her wet, and although it was a turnoff, she had to stick to the plan and make him feel like he was some sort of super-sex hero.

Tomeka watched as he stroked the head of his member, wanting to speed up the process. She seductively walked back to the couch, kneeled down, and cuffed his balls in her hand. She started stroking them like she was kneading fresh, homemade biscuit dough.

Danny's member was a nice size if it would stay hard long enough. Tomeka felt she could have an hour of fun with it. She felt it was a waste of dick because it couldn't stay hard long enough to please her. She was going to try to work with what she had in front of her. She tried to get it back hard, even if it didn't last long.

"Come on, Meka. A nigga just had to get that first one off," Danny said with a little desperation in his voice. He could see the disappointment in Tomeka's face. He stroked faster to get his member to stand at attention once again.

"Yeah, that's what you said before, but the shit ain't work out. I don't have time to be wasting, Danny. To be honest, I kind of like you. At first, I was only fuckin' with you because of the promise you made me—to make me wifey when you take Jamir's ass out—but even if you don't succeed in your plan, I still hope to have something with you." Tomeka softened her tone just enough to get Danny to trust her some more.

"Don't worry about my plan. I'm gonna succeed because of that shit that happened with Raw. That nigga got plenty of trust in me now, and because of it, he gonna finally let me in deeper. Once I get all the information I need, I'm going to bury his ass, and your pretty ass gonna be right beside me every step of the way. Think you can handle that? Being a baller's wifey takes a lot of work."

"You ain't said shit. I already clocked in and don't mind doing overtime. Whatever you need me to do, I'ma do it with no questions asked. All you gotta do is say the word."

"Well, right now, I need you to go back to work on this dick. Let a nigga show you what overtime pays."

Tomeka gave a slight smirk and got busy. She didn't care if it took all night to be sure Danny was fully pleased if he continued to think that he was in control. She had to admit she was having a little fun. It wasn't as much as she would have liked, but it wasn't that bad. The only downside was that Danny couldn't make her cum.

She finally told him that she had to piss. Once she went into the bathroom and shut the door, she lifted her right leg and planted it on the side of the tub. Tomeka fingered herself and played with her clit until she came. It didn't take her long, because it had already built up inside her. She had already made up her mind to find another source of pleasure because Danny wasn't hitting it on it. She hoped he would hurry up and reveal his whole plan so she could move on.

Tomeka breathed a sigh of relief and wiped herself off. Once she grabbed the doorknob, she rolled her eyes toward the ceiling to get herself back into the role she had to play while half fucking Danny. The ability to switch up roles was all thanks to Raw. She had to play a role for so long until she had naturally good acting skills.

When she walked back to the room, Danny was on the phone. She wasn't an envious type of female, but if she found out he was talking to another female and hadn't even finished the job with her, she was gonna curse him all the way out.

She seductively walked in front of him and began to play with her nipples to see what type of reaction he would give her. If he didn't respond to her freakiness in the right way, there would be hell to pay because the female that should've been on his mind right then was her.

"Oh, yes. Go 'head, Meka. Do that freaky shit, baby." He spoke in a raspy growl.

Tomeka realized she didn't have anything to envy. She smacked her lips and sat down beside him. She couldn't lie to herself for real. She wondered who was on the other end of that call. As soon as he ended the call, she got all into his business.

"I know good and well you ain't talking to your bitch while you here in my shit, Danny."

"Girl, just chill out. That was Jamir, and if it would have been my bitch, what you gonna do about it?"

"Hm, I was gonna let that hoe know that you ain't need her no more. This pussy got you on lock now."

"Oh, yeah? That's what you think? Meka, just so you know, I ain't found a pussy yet that can lock me down, so don't waste your time trying. You can be wifey, but a nigga got other priorities, so I keep my options open."

With that said, Danny got up and got dressed. He then gathered his things, tapped Tomeka on the ass, and walked out, leaving her pissed, with no explanation at all. He was on a mission, and he couldn't allow her to stop him from fulfilling it.

Chapter 3

The thick red bone had her hand on the back of Jamir's neck, giving him some balance while she ground her thong-clad pussy against the seam of his black Gucci jeans. The bitch was fine, and he noticed her when he first went into the club. He paid her for a nice song and the lap dance, but she couldn't manage to get him excited. It wasn't because she hadn't been good at what she was doing, but because his concentration was elsewhere.

Jamir finally put his hands under her armpits and lifted her off him. She scrunched her eyebrows together and gave him a confused look because she thought she had been doing her thing. The red bone put her hands on her hips and tried to figure out what was going on. She wasn't bold enough to ask him. She knew Jamir didn't owe her an explanation. She wasn't his bitch.

She turned her head in the direction he was looking and caught a quick attitude, but instead of going off on him, she did the smart thing and walked away. Jamir hadn't even noticed the red bone was gone, because he was no longer focused on her. He made his way across the room to the brown-skinned dancer he had his eyes on.

She stood over a light-skinned brother with shoulder-length dreads and a mouthful of gold teeth. Jamir watched as she rotated her hips like she was riding a big dick while the dread rubbed between her legs. She didn't look like she was new to what she was doing, which made Jamir wonder just how long she had been at it. That question would have to wait, though, because Jamir had other concerns. He was on her so fast that the nigga in front of her didn't even realize it until her hips stopped moving. Erica turned her head, and once she saw that it was Jamir, she caught an instant attitude.

"Damn you, Jamir. What the hell are you doing here? Shouldn't you be somewhere feeding crack to that crackhead you got sniffing up your ass instead of in here making problems for me?"

"I don't give a damn about what you doing in here, shaking your asses for random muthafuckas. All I wanna know is where my daughter at while you doin' this shit." Before Erica had a chance to answer, the dread-headed dude stood.

He went to reach for his piece, but Jamir moved a little quicker than he did. The dreaded man held his hands up in surrender because, honestly, he hadn't gone there for a gunplay. He'd only wanted to kick back and have a good time. He enjoyed watching the dancers shake their asses for some paper. He respected the hustle and never tried to knock on it. However, he didn't know the deal with the dancer and the nigga that had a gun pointed at him, but he wasn't about to get caught in the middle of it.

"Hey, bro. I ain't come here looking for trouble. I'm just trying to have a good time, feel on a little pussy, and maybe get into a little something. That's all."

Jamir nodded his head to motion for the dread head to sit back down. Once he was seated, Jamir backed up and put his gun away. He turned his head and looked at Erica with disgust. He didn't know why he had expected anything different, because he knew she was a hoe from the first day he met her, and leopards didn't change their spots. Yet he stuck his dick into her anyway. There wasn't shit he could do to change it. That was done for him, and now he had problems he didn't need.

Jamir reached out and grabbed Erica by the arm, pulling her closer to him. He looked up and down at her half-naked body and shook his head.

He remembered all the reasons he had fucked with her in the first place. But now, the mere sight of her made him sick to his stomach. He hadn't messed with her in a while and was glad he made that choice. He swore to himself, no matter what, he would never touch her again.

"The fuck is wrong with you? What type of example you up in here making! My daughter needs a lady to look up to, not a damn hoe."

"Oh, you mean a lady like that white bitch you be fuckin' with? Spare me with that bullshit, Jamir. And as far as our daughter is concerned, I don't do no so-called hoe shit nowhere near her. I'm a damn good mother and will and have sacrificed my life for her. But you, her father, so busy sniffing in a crackhead's ass, you can't even manage to spend any time with your daughter. Jamir, you such a hypocrite."

"Erica, you are still on that shit. It's all good, though. Do I need to remind you that the only reason you are still breathing is because of that little girl? Fuck what I'm doing. She came out yo' pussy, and if something happens to her, it's gonna all be on you. I promise."

"Oh, yeah? Well, unless you gonna step up and be a daddy to her, your best bet is to step off and get the fuck on like you been doin'."

Jamir stared into Erica's eyes while his nose flared in anger. He didn't want to admit it, but she was right. He hardly ever spent any time with his little girl, and even though he provided for her abundantly, he knew it wasn't enough. She needed her daddy, but Jamir chose the streets over time with her. He told himself he would try to make some changes, but he knew it would never matter either way.

The sound of Danny's voice caused Jamir to let Erica's arm go. He had almost forgotten about him but quickly remembered he'd asked him to meet up with him. Erica and her drama would have to wait 'til another time because he had more important shit to deal with.

"'Sup, bruh? Why you wasting energy on the broad? Hoe ain't even worth it."

Jamir turned to face Danny and gave him some dap before dismissing Erica, who rolled her eyes. Then she covered her bare breasts as though she had suddenly become embarrassed.

Jamir shook his head and gave her one final warning. "You's a lucky bitch tonight. But when I come through to see my seed, I'ma put a foot in that ass," he warned.

"Whatever, Jamir. Just make sure my nigga ain't there when you pull up. Wouldn't want you to get fucked up."

Jamir didn't pay that shit no mind. He had a few homies who lived on the same block as Erica. That was the main reason he had moved her there. He wondered why none of them had mentioned that she had been stripping and leaving his daughter to be tended to by someone else. He told himself he would make it his business to swing by there and see what the hell was really going on. First, he had other things on his agenda.

***

"'Sup, D? Thanks for meeting me. I figured, with this new turn of events, we could meet up, talk some business, and maybe luck up on some entertainment from hoes. You cool with that?"

"You damn right, playboy! Shit, a nigga could always use some enjoyment and business at the moment."

"Say less. Come on. I already grabbed us a table."

Jamir led Danny to the small, round table he had been sitting at before he saw Erica. No sooner than they sat down, the waitress, skimpily clad in a pair of boy shorts and a tank top, approached them, and she smiled at Jamir, who'd just ignored her, so she was taking her chances with Danny.

"Hey, handsome. What can I get for you tonight?"

Danny looked at her smooth, peanut-butter-colored skin and smiled. Her hips were wide, and her thighs were thick. As he imagined being between them, he felt his manhood rise. What he wanted from her wasn't on the menu, but he gave it his best shot.

"Well, unless I can get yo' fine as on a platter, then I'm good."

"Hmm, I think I can honor that request. Why don't you meet me in the ladies' room in ten minutes?"

"Shit, consider me there already." Danny was eager to see what that body could do.

The waitress looked directly at Jamir and smirked sexily before she walked away to prepare herself for what she believed to be a massive dick down. She hoped Danny was about to glue her.

"Nigga, you know you crazy as hell. You don't even know that bitch. You think you're the only muthafucka she done tried to throw some pussy at?"

"Fuck you mean? That's some free pussy right there. I'll be a damned fool if I pass up on that."

"Hey, all I'm saying is, when it's free, there's usually gonna be something that ain't right about it. You better watch that shit."

"Good lookin' out, bro. I hear you, but don't worry. I got this."

"If you say so. But I need to talk to you about something else first. I'll be honest with you. I ain't never been too keen on trusting muthafuckas, not even you. However, you made me see that I've been wrong about you by showing me. Yo, word, you saved me from that bullshit when Raw had been plottin'. I can't believe I had a snake at the table wit' me the whole time. But you looked out for me, and I appreciate it. I could never repay you for that, but what I can do is show you how grateful I am by setting you up on your own block. You can get whoever you want and build a nice crew to run it.

Plus, it will keep you out of the streets so you can stay home and spend more time with Trish and your seed. A growing baby boy like that needs Daddy around. You good with that?"

"You serious, Mir? I mean, damn. We've been cool a long time, but I ain't never expected you to bless me like this."

"Come on, D. You deserve it. The little shit I was throwing your way was mere crumbs compared to what I'm about to put in your hands. You ain't never spoke too much about it, but I know you be struggling sometimes to provide for Trish and your son. You should be living large with no worries, and I'm about to make sure that happens for you. Those days of struggling are over, my boy. I give you my word on that."

"Thanks, bro. This shit coming at me right on time. I ain't told you this yet, but Trish is pregnant again."

"Ohh yeah? Congratulations then. But if you don't start keeping that muthafucka in your jeans, she ain't gonna be the only one."

Both of them shared a laugh because they both knew Danny dished out dick like scoops of ice cream. It was a miracle he hadn't caught any STDs, or worse, AIDS, because he hated wearing condoms. Jamir learned his lesson from that one slip-up with Erica, and other than Rachel, he didn't take any more chances.

"Don't worry, Mir. I'm gonna chill one day. Just not today. I got that fine ass honey waiting in the bathroom for me, so what I'm about to do is go hit it real quick, and then I'll consider taking a break. I'll be back."

He stood up and rushed away from the table as if getting to the female who was waiting for him in the bathroom was an emergency. Jamir already knew he wouldn't be gone for long, but in that situation, it might have been a good thing. Jamir had never met a muthafucka so anxious to dip in some strange pussy, and he truly believed, one day, Danny's indiscretions would catch up with him. But that wasn't

Jamir's problem, so he decided to sit back and relax while the honeys performed and did their thing.

He felt he needed to focus on someone else because he was still trying to get over the fact that Erica had been up in that very place, shaking her ass. He knew that bitch was ratchet, and nothing would ever change that. He just hoped his daughter didn't turn out to be just like her.

Jamir suddenly turned his thoughts to his mother. He wondered if she had ever regretted leaving him and Missy with their grandmother so she could run off with a man who wasn't their father. It had been a fucked-up situation, but thankfully, he and Missy turned out ok.

He still couldn't believe Missy was gone. He thought about her every day and vowed to keep asking questions until he found out the person who led her down the road to her death. He wouldn't rest until he led them down the same road.

Jamir had been so deep in his thoughts that he didn't realize Danny had sat back down beside him until he felt a tap on his shoulder.

"Damn, Mir. Where the hell your mind went? I've been sitting here calling your name and shit, but your mind is clearly somewhere else".

"Ohh, sorry about that, D. I was just sitting here thinking about how far we have come and all the shit we had to go through to get here. It's just crazy, bro. Some things, we gained, but so much has been lost. I mean, look at Missy— she supposed to be here right now, but she gone, man. And she ain't never coming back. Without her, a nigga sometimes feel like I ain't got nobody if it wasn't for you, D. I'll be all alone in this game, man. Real talk."

"Well, don't worry, Jamir. I'm always here, bro. Ain't a damned thing changed about that. You my nigga, and I'm always gonna hold you down. As for Missy, we're gonna find out what happened, and we're gonna take them muthafuckas out. That's my word."

"Thanks, D. Good to hear. Now let's get us some of this honey over here to enjoy. We work hard for this money, right? Might as well use it on something nice."

"Hell yeah, that's what I'm talking about."

As soon as Jamir said it, two fine honeys walked over to them—one dark chocolate, the other pure porcelain. The two of them locked their eyes with Danny and Jamir and then put on a hell of a show. However, no matter how good their performance was, Jamir couldn't shake the thoughts of Missy; he couldn't wait to avenge her death. He just didn't know how close her killer really was.

Chapter 4

Tomeka had taken a nice, long shower and lay down for the night. She was a little hyped, so she decided to give herself an orgasm, just a little something to help her fall asleep faster. She was exhausted, but she knew sleep wouldn't come easily. It never did for her, but with a little assistance, she would go straight into dreamland and sleep like a baby.

She positioned herself just right and then spread her legs, but as soon as she placed her middle finger over her clit, a knock sounded at the door. Tomeka closed her eyes and pressed down on her swollen bud, trying to ignore whoever it was disturbing her groove. They were persistent and continued to knock.

She finally gave up on her sexual mission and got out of bed, threw a long sleep shirt over her naked body, and went to give them a piece of her mind. She hadn't been expecting anyone and knew it couldn't have been Danny-Two-Minutes back to waste her time. If it was, she had a mind to curse his black ass all the way out because, honestly, she wasn't in the mood for company.

Tomeka enjoyed spending time by herself. That's why, apart from Raw's house, she had her own place. That was also why she only dated dope boys. They were the ones who would always be out in the streets, while their women stayed home and chilled. Plus, she liked that she didn't have to hold down a job. A street nigga took care of his bitch and gave her everything she desired. Her mama taught her that at a young age, long before Tomeka even knew what a street nigga was. But when she found out, she was on a mission to get her one. If he didn't wear Drop Sports, have a bunch of tattoos, or carry a loaded nine with a bankroll in his pocket, they didn't stand a chance, and that was the way it would always be.

Tomeka walked barefoot through her living room. Her small feet sank into the plush carpet with every step she took. Only a dim light coming from over the kitchen's stove led her way, but even without it, the short distance was nothing for her to track. She had done it so many times before when Raw would knock on the door late at night instead of opting to go to her house. She liked the fact that Tomeka's little hideout was close to the block she served on, so she didn't have to drive far to get a good night's sleep. It was also quicker for her to get away when the block was hot, which was more often than not.

Tomeka had never been a scary bitch, so she wasn't worried about who was on the other side of the door. She didn't even bother to look out the peephole before she opened it, but once she saw who it was, she regretted that decision.

Before Tomeka even had time to blink, Blount had his gloved hand wrapped around her neck. She had thought nothing of him because he had been out of town for a family funeral and had been gone for a minute. However, Tomeka should have known once he came back, he would look for Raw, and when he couldn't find her, he would ask a lot of questions.

Blount and Raw had been best friends for as long as the hood could remember. They were more like brother and sister and always had each other's backs. Blount knew something was wrong when Raw didn't reach out to him. Blount knew that there was no way Raw wouldn't have checked up on him, especially knowing he was saying goodbye to the woman who raised him. Blount had to push the bad feelings aside and deal with them when he got back in town. Someone owed him some answers, and he wasn't leaving Tomeka's without them.

"Bitch, where the fuck is my partner at? And you better not even think of lying to me."

Tomeka was trying to pry Blount's hand from around her neck, but his grip was solid, so she did the only thing she could and went limp. Thankfully, it worked, and Blount let go and let her fall to the floor. He knew she wasn't dead, but it wasn't because he didn't want her to be. Blount couldn't stand Tomeka and always told Raw that she would be her downfall.

Blount locked the front door and pulled out his nine-millimeter. He looked down at her pathetic attempt to play dead, but Blount was a killer, and he knew when a bitch had expired at his hands. He laughed and shook his head as he kneeled in front of her, frowning with disgust. He examined her from head to toe. The shirt she had on barely covered her naked flesh, but it didn't turn him on in the least. Her pussy had been run through like a bike tunnel by many, even before Raw pulled her. She would never be more than a washed-up hoe to Blount, and now that he suspected some foul shit in Raw's disappearance, he would show her no mercy.

Blount grabbed Tomeka by the ankle and began to drag her into the living room. Suddenly, she began to kick, but she was wasting her time because he wasn't letting her go. When Blount got to the couch, he sat down with Tomeka's ankle still in his grip. He began questioning her again. One way or another, this bitch was going to answer him.

"So, you wanna play dead, bitch? Huh? You must don' forgot who the fuck I am. Meka, you know what I'm capable of. Now, I'ma ask you one mo' time. Where is Raw?" His voice boomed throughout her house with so much anger.

Tomeka knew this situation at this moment was serious. She knew Blount hated her and didn't give a damn about her pretty looks or thick thighs. She knew Blount didn't show mercy to anyone, not even women or children. He was all business, and he wasn't any different this time, so she thought carefully about what her next move would be. Tomeka tried anyway, through teary eyes, to plead her case with him because if he knew what happened, she was for sure dead, so she played dumbfounded as to what was going on.

"I-I-I don't know where she is. We had a falling out that didn't end well. I haven't seen her or heard from her since. That's the truth. For all I know, she's probably between another hoe's thighs as we speak. Pac-Man-ass nigga."

Blount shook his head because he knew Tomeka was lying to him. The bitch knew something though, and he would make her confess one way or another. "So that's gonna be your final answer, huh?"

"Uh, yeah. It's my only answer because it's the truth. I ain't got no reason to lie to you."

Even in the face of death, Tomeka stayed strong. Her mother always told her never to show weakness to any man.

Blount shrugged his shoulders and smiled at Tomeka. At this point, she was accepting her fate. Whatever way it played out, she was gonna answer it on her terms. She had gotten over on many niggas throughout her life, but she must not have known that Blount wasn't the average nigga. Her words didn't mean shit to him, and neither did her life. Blount gripped her ankle even tighter and grabbed her foot with his other hand. It was time to do what he loved most, and that was make a bitch tell it all.

"Oh! Oh, shit!" Tomeka yelled in pain as she felt her bones begin to snap at the ankle. At that moment, she became one of those weak ass females she hated, and if she didn't tell Blount quickly, he would snap the other ankle, too. He could give two fucks about her. All he wanted was to know where Raw was.

"Told me the truth, huh? Bitch, you ain't told me shit. You know how I get down, so I don't know why you are testing me. You know you don't mean a damn thing to me. So, if I have to stay here all night and break every fuckin' bone in your body, I will. Now I'm gonna give you another chance, and if you don't tell me what I want to know, you gonna wake up tomorrow in a full-body cast, if you wake up at all."

Tomeka grabbed her ankle and lay there. In pain, with streams of tears rolling down her cheeks, she knew that she would rather for him to go ahead and kill her and get it over with. But Tomeka knew that wasn't going to happen. Blount liked to make people suffer, and she didn't want that. She contemplated her next words and then decided it would be best to give him what he wanted. Before she had a chance to speak, Blount grabbed her other ankle.

"Wait, wait, please, Blount! I'll tell you! It was Danny. He shot Raw right in the head. I was hiding in the closet and saw him do it. He didn't know I was there, so he don't even know that I saw him. That's the truth."

"Wait, what? Danny? Do you mean that black ass muthafucka that be with Jamir? I thought we had all got on the same page. What happened with that?"

Tomeka nodded through a flow of tears that sealed Danny's fate. She didn't give a damn about him anyway. His sex game was short, and his pockets were shallow. She felt he would never make it to boss status, and getting him out of the way would only make the world a better place. Also, with him out of the way would make it easier for her to get to Jamir. Tomeka decided not to mention what really happened because she would have to implicate herself, and she needed to make sure Blount saw her as a victim, too.

"Yes, Blount, that Danny. I thought y'all had become cool. At least, that was what it looked like to me. I remember Raw telling me about some beef they had over a bitch some years back. But Danny acted like he had let it go. He somehow had Raw and Jamir fooled and only played nice so he could get close to them. Now Raw's gone, and she was all I had. What I'm gon' to do without her, man?"

Watching her crocodile tears, Blount did not feel the least bit sorry for Tomeka and couldn't care less about her tears, because something in his gut told him she was hiding something else. He felt, somehow, she handed him what she wanted him to hear, but he decided he would deal with Danny first. He could always come back and take care of this bitch later. In the meantime, though, Blount felt he had to ensure himself she wouldn't pull a quick move and skip town on him. He looked down at her while she held on to the ankle he had already broken and reached out to grab the other one. He'd be damned if she got away from him.

"No! No! What are you doing, Blount? I already told you what I know."

"Nah, nah, Meka. Something ain't addin' up. I think you only told me what you wanted me to know, for some reason. I feel like that ain't the whole story. So, until I find out the whole truth, I gotta do what I gotta do to make sure your ass don't snake off and leave town in case I gotta come back and see you. Ya feel me?"

Before Tomeka could get out another word, Blount twisted her other ankle. The bone snapped even louder than the first, and the pain took Tomeka's breath away. She couldn't even scream and knew, even if she had, no one would hear her and come to her rescue. Because she had soundproofed the walls in her apartment, Tomeka was on her own.

She lay as still as she could on the floor and cried, holding her limp ankles. She had never had a broken bone in her body before, so that type of pain was new to her, and she didn't know what to do. Blount stood up and looked down at her. His only thoughts were of Raw. She had been his partner for so long, and there was no one else who could replace her.

Blount grew up as an only child, and Raw was like both a brother and a sister to him. He was able to talk about his beef with niggas and his issues with the bitches because Raw lived on both sides. Blount swore to himself that whatever he did from that day on, he would do it in her memory. He would never let her name be forgotten in the streets or his heart.

Blount's heart was broken, and all he could do was shake his head in disbelief that his sister was really gone. Then he stepped over Tomeka like she was just another piece of trash that had been thrown in the streets. There was something more important that he needed to tend to, and he refused to waste another minute on her. But as soon as he put his hand on the doorknob, he heard her cry out to him.

"Blount, wait, please! I need to go to the hospital! How am I supposed to get there?"

With a mean scowl, Blount looked back at Tomeka and smiled. Her pain didn't affect him at all, but it was only right to answer her question since it was, after all, he who put her in that position.

"Well, Tomeka, I guess you're gonna have to get up and walk your ass there. You stupid bitch." He continued out the door, leaving Tomeka in pain and fear.

Chapter 5

Danny woke up with a killer headache. His head pounded like someone had taken a hammer to it. The bright sun shining through his window almost blinded him. As he quickly opened his eyes, he closed them right back. He thought back to last night. Then he remembered and smiled.

He hadn't had his dick sucked that good in a while. He told himself he would go back and find the bitch that made him cum like a running faucet. However, what he didn't predict was that he wouldn't have to go very far. Danny could feel warm lips and a long tongue making circular motions around the head of his manhood. He was afraid to open his eyes because if it was a dream, he didn't want it to end. He moaned in delight as he felt the tip of his manhood touch the back of her tonsils. He enjoyed the pleasure of the treatment he was getting at this moment.

"Oh, shit. Suck this dick, baby," he managed to groggily say as the head job was getting good. Feeling his manhood getting wetter, he tried to fight the feeling and not cum too fast, but just like any other time, he couldn't hold back, and he released his load in under two minutes.

Hearing the person giggle, he managed to squint and then open his eyes all the way. He was relieved it was the same female from the night before as she wiped her chin of his seeds.

"Hey, big guy. Just thought I would get breakfast out of the way," she said, smiling.

"Yeah, sorry about the quickness. That shit felt so good, especially with the morning nut. It always catches me off guard."

"Don't worry about it. I don't mind it being quick, because this bitch right here have enough skill to keep it coming back-to-back. Besides a good, hard dick is rare these days. Most pretty boys like you always come up short, if you know what I mean."

Her flirting caused Danny's ego to swell. He had his fair share of women, and they always seemed to complain about how fast he nutted, but it was refreshing and flattering to finally meet someone who appreciated his sex game. That was when he decided she was a keeper. He didn't like sharing, so eventually, he was gonna have to have her quit the club. He didn't want his main bitch or his side bitch to share his pussy.

He was so gone in the head, he hadn't even remembered her name. "What's yo' name, shawty?"

"My name is Cassie, short for Cassandra. Why? What, you wanna be my Puff Daddy?"

He laughed at her little joke. He found her really amusing, and she gave out good vibes. He needed someone to run to when Trish's ass got out of hand, which was quite often. It was just a little breath of fresh air, and Cassie was definitely going to be that.

"Ohh, ok, Cassie, short for Cassandra, that was cute, but Puff Daddy ain't got shit on me. How you feel about quitting that club and only dancing on this dick? Can't have you up in there showing my shit to other niggas. You're gonna have to be all mine."

"Quitting the club? I don't know, big fella. Quitting the club, that ain't nothing for me to do. I ain't like working there anyway. I was just doing what I had to do to survive. Besides, them are some hating ass hoes up in there. Plus, the patrons are so disrespectful at times, so I don't mind walking away from them, but only if it's worth it."

"Ok, Miss Cassandra. That's cool, but I gotta let you know upfront that I got a baby mama, and her ass be trippin' on a nigga. I'm gonna need you to play your position without all that drama. You think you can do that?"

"I'm good at playing positions, baby. As long as you feed me that good dick and give me what I need, I'll play anywhere on any field you'd like."

Danny smiled and nodded his head at her because there wasn't nothing better than a bitch you could control. Talking to Cassie made him think of Missy. At times, he found himself missing her, just not enough to cry about it. Missy had started to get too deep in her feelings, making Danny paranoid. He hated to imagine what would have happened if she had slipped up and told Jamir about their affair; they would have been at war for sure, and he definitely wouldn't have been where he was.

Feeling the vibration from his cell phone broke Danny from his thoughts. He almost forgot that Cassie was still there, but she giggled and reminded him. He looked over at her and then grabbed his limp manhood. He felt like he still had another round in him, but before he had a chance to act on it, his cell phone vibrated again.

"It's been buzzing like that all night, but I'm not the type of bitch to answer a nigga's phone. That's not my place. You had better check it, though. It might be important."

Danny put his legs on one side of the bed so he could sit up. His cell phone was still on the floor beside his jeans where he'd left it, proving that Cassie was telling the truth. When Danny picked it up and checked the caller ID, he saw that it was Trish. But instead of answering, he sent her straight to voicemail. He noticed that she had been calling him back-to-back all night, but he still ignored her pleas to answer. Not wanting to be bothered anymore, Danny went ahead and turned his phone off, and he turned back to Cassie.

"Ain't nothin' she want that important, but I'll tell you what it is—that ass. So go ahead and boot it up. I got something real special for you."

Cassie was obedient and did just what Danny told her. She couldn't wait to see what he had in store for her. She had to admit that he was at her level, and she liked his style. She wasn't worried about his baby mama because she planned to take up as much of his time as possible, until all of his time became hers.

Cassie noticed that Danny had pulled out a small baggie of cocaine and smiled. She knew exactly what he was going to do with it, because when it came to sexual experiences, there wasn't shit she hadn't tried. She felt the tingle instantly when Danny reached between her thighs and rubbed the white powder in the middle of them.

He then poured a little bit on the head of his dick and pushed it inside of her. Within seconds, he was sweating from the force he used to pound into her and wasn't about to let up.

When it was all over, Danny was amazed at himself because he fucked Cassie for over five minutes before he came. As embarrassing as it was, he admitted that was the longest he'd ever gone for. That was why he planned to keep Cassie around for a long time. She was the first female that he had ever met and made him feel like a man. Plus, the pussy was good. The best part of it all, though, was the fact she didn't mind playing the sidepiece.

After their fuck fest was finally over, Danny decided to turn his phone back on just in case Jamir tried to get a hold of him. As soon as the device lit up, he noticed Trish had tried to call him again. He really wasn't in the mood to hear her bitching but pressed the call back button anyway. When she didn't answer her phone, he was pissed and threw his phone back on the floor. The nerve of her to blow his phone up all night and then not answer when he called her back infuriated him. He would make sure to straighten her ass out when he got home. But in the meantime, he just wanted to ease his mind.

"What's the matter, Danny? Yo' baby momma didn't answer?"

Danny just shook his head and looked at her. Something inside him felt very strange. Trish not answering after she had called him all night with no answer—even if she answered the phone only to curse him out—it wasn't like her, not answering at all. He just couldn't place what it was, so he brushed the feeling away and kissed Cassie on the forehead.

"She just acting shady 'cause I didn't come home, is all. She'll be alright, though. I have been dealing with this shit for a long time, so I know how this gonna play out. I know how to handle her ass. I'll make it there eventually, but for the moment, I'm here with you, catching me some calm before the storm. I need this peace, so I'm not gonna let that disturb what me and you entertaining at the moment."

"Well, don't worry about that, baby. I'll always bring you a little peace, as long as you keep throwing me that big piece." She laughed.

Cassie lay her head on his chest and closed her eyes to take a much-needed nap, but Danny couldn't sleep. His mind was in too many other places. He was still stuck on the fact that Trish never answered the phone after calling him all night that many times.

He tried to shake this bad feeling he had, but it wouldn't go away. He lay there with Cassie lying on his chest as he held her close, not knowing that the feelings he was feeling would be far worse than he could have ever imagined.

Chapter 6

Jamir drove from block to block on a mission to locate Danny, but it was as if he had turned ghost on him. He had even tried to call him several times, but all those calls went unanswered. He knew Danny was probably somewhere deep in some pussy because Jamir couldn't think of anything else. That would keep him from answering. If Danny hadn't responded yet, then he knew he wasn't going to.

Jamir finally grew frustrated and gave up his search. He had money to make and had wasted enough time. He couldn't afford to waste any more. Besides, he was sure Danny had already seen the news.

Jameer pulled up beside Old Man Nat's and parked in his usual spot. It was still a little early, but the fiends had already begun to show their faces. Jamir had always been shocked at the people who threw their hard-earned money away for ten seconds of a high. Some of them held high-level jobs, working sixty-hour weeks, only to turn around and blow their paycheck on some cooked-up cocaine? Jamir had to admit that he respected the fact that they could hold down a nine-to-five job; however, at the end of the day, it was all for nothing.

"Jamir? Say? Jamir?"

Jamir heard someone call his name in a low whisper, so he waited to make sure he wasn't losing his mind and see if he would hear it again. Then, just a little louder than before, he heard, "Hey, Jamir. Over here by the tree. It's me."

Jamir turned his head toward the tree, only to see Rita peeping from behind. Every time she smoked crack, she became paranoid. In her mind, she could swear people were looking for her.

She would hide behind anything she could until she realized the coast was clear. Rita had been a crackhead for a long time—as long as Jamir had known her—and that was a long time.

Being an addict seemed to fit her, though, and she acted like she never wanted to do anything different. Rita sucked every nigga's dick that worked on the block and even some who came in from out of town. She didn't care where the dick had been or how long it had been since it had been there. She was just nasty like that. Rita had even sucked Danny's dick around the corner one night. She told everybody it was the quickest twenty dollars she'd ever made and would often look for him when she had run out of options.

"Damn, Rita. The hell you doing behind the tree, man? Somebody looking for you or something?"

"Somebody always looking for me because they know ain't nan other bitch out here gonna give it to them like me. They say I'm the best that ever did it. You should never take someone else's word. How about you be the judge of it and test it out for yourself?"

"Hell no. My dick ain't going nowhere near you. I'd rather let Edward Scissorhands jack my shit off first."

"That's real fucked up, Jamir, but it's all good. I was looking for Danny anyway. I ain't been seeing much of him lately. I heard about what happened last night. That was real fucked up what they did."

"Yeah, it was fucked up. The sad thing is, I don't think Danny knows yet. I can't even reach his ass."

"Hey, that means he probably with some bitch, holed up in that motel. I could take a walk and see can I find them if you want."

"Thanks, Rita, but he'll show up when he shows up, and in the meantime, there's a little something to hold you off."

Jamir pulled out a baggie full of crack, shaking his head when he noticed Rita lick her lips. He wondered when the last time she had eaten, or the last time she even bathed. He couldn't believe that she had let herself go the way she had. See really used to be the finest bitch walking, even on that shit.

One day, she smoked a bad batch and somehow lost what little bit of respect she had left. Once she lost that, everyone else lost theirs for her, too. Her breasts, which were once plump and juicy, were now saggy, and her ass had so much cellulite in it, it looked like a road full of potholes.

But a dick didn't have a conscience and would run up in anything open.

Rita wrapped her fist around it as tightly as she could. She wasn't used to someone giving her dope for nothing, but Jamir had always been a different type of dude, and she appreciated that. Rita smiled and turned, then began to walk away, but Jamir stopped her.

"Hey, Rita? You seen Rachel around here anywhere?"

"Rachel got picked up by the law for some checks she wrote. She probably gon' be goin' to prison for a while. They said she wrote a whole book of them. Why are you asking about her anyway? You got to thang for her?"

"Nah, I just wonder why I haven't seen her in a while— that's all."

"Yeah, ok. You seem a little disappointed about that, but it ain't my business. What is my business is these lil' pieces of heaven you just gave me. They callin' me, and when they do, I like to answer, so see ya." She quickly walked off, leaving Jamir with his thoughts. She hadn't been gone for two minutes before another voice caught him completely off guard.

"Damn, Jamir. Please tell me you ain't hittin' that? I hear she fire with that shit, and I would hate to see you go out like that."

"Hell nah. I ain't neva had it and don't want it. Sup wit' you, Barnes? What brings you out this way?"

"Get my hands in the real estate game. I figured I'd come out to the neighborhood and check out some houses. I found a couple I'm thinking about investing in, you know, just a little extra security for my future."

"Real estate, huh? Well, how you end up back here talking to me? I hope you ain't checking for Rachel, because she ain't gonna be around for a while."

"Jamir, what you don't know about me is that I keep my word. You ain't gotta worry about your girl, because she ain't on my radar anymore. I told you I would keep my distance, and I meant that. I was actually hoping that I could talk about some business with you, but if you ain't up for turning that change you make into big faces, then I guess I'll be on my way. I'm always certain I can find someone else who wants to make it to the top. Not saying you ain't climbing, but I can push you well above where you at now, just a little quicker, though."

Jamir wasn't sure if what Jason said was an insult or not. He didn't want to misjudge the conversation, because the last thing he needed was to make another enemy when he had yet to get rid of the ones he already had. He decided it was best to push the offense out of his mind and see just what Jason Barnes was talking about.

"I'm doing alright, but I always aim to do better. What you got in mind?"

"I got a hundred kilos I need picked up. Twenty-five will go to you for the trouble."

"What's wrong with you picking them up, or better yet, one of your mules. Why you coming to me?"

"See, that's what makes me different than other muthafuckas in the game. I don't use others as a sacrifice.

What type of man would I be if I send someone else to do my dirty work? I feel that if I'm man enough to put my foot in the game, then I should be man enough to walk the road. I do the crime; it's my place to do the time. So far, I've been blessed, and I'ma keep going until I run out of gas. That's how it should be. Also, I can't leave town right now. My mom is in Hospice, on her deathbed, and I wouldn't be able to live with myself if I ain't there when she shuts her eyes for the last and final time. Doctors say she ain't got long, like she ain't gonna make it 'til the end of the week. I ain't never trusted anyone to handle my shit, but I know you are legit and thorough. You gonna take care of mine as if it were your own."

"Right about that, and I'm sorry to hear about your old girl. I do need a little time, though, to think about it. I'll get back to you when I make my decision, alright?"

"That's real, but I'm gonna need the answer before daybreak so I can handle all of the arrangements. Ernesto likes for shit to be done properly and without any issues. I've been fucking with him without any issues since I was a jit. He gave me my first break, and I ain't even gonna lie. I ain't have the first clue of what to do with it.

"He took his time, though, and showed me everything I needed to do. Got nothing but love and respect for that man. I need to send someone in my place who is going to show him the same thing—the respect that he deserves. So, here's my number. Let me know what you decide. I'll be waiting for your call."

Jamir smirked and grabbed the small piece of paper from Jason's hand. He gave it a glance and put it in his pocket. Jason smiled and walked away, somehow already certain of what Jamir would decide. The two of them had more in common than they could have imagined, and if they had joined teams by now, they would have been a force to be reckoned with.

Jamir sat and thought about what Jason had said. One hundred kilos was a lot of cocaine to pack up and ride down the highway with. But it wouldn't be the first time he'd taken such a chance. Jamir didn't really need the twenty-five keys, but he kept the business to himself. He already had a foreign connection, but only two people knew about it.

He and his connect, Malcolm, had once been in the loop, but Jamir told him he had cut ties with the foreigner. Malcolm never asked any questions and never brought the subject up again.

The vibration of a cell phone brought Jamir back to reality. When he saw that it was Danny, he quickly answered. He could tell his partner was upset. Jamir knew he had already heard the news.

"What's up, D? You alright?"

"Man, Mir-Mir, they gone. Trish and my babies are gone. She been calling me back-to-back, and I ain't even answered her. Bro, I ain't even get to say goodbye."

"Danny, my nigga. We gonna find out what happened, and we gonna respond to whoever did that to her. In the meantime, you gotta stay up and make sure you send them to their final resting place in peace. I could only imagine the pain you're going through. When I heard it on the news, I was trying to get at you to see if I could help. Man, bro, this fucked up."

"All those nights she just wanted me to come home, and I ain't even go. I was too busy with some other bitch, and now I can't ever go home to her again. What I'm gon' do, man? What I'm going to do without her? What about my son and my daughter? They didn't even get a chance, man, to live life."

"I'm here for you, D, but you can't sit around and drown yourself in regrets. What's done is done, and you can't take it back. But you gotta keep pushing and keep their memory alive. Remember what you told me when I lost Missy? That shit applies to you, too. I got you, my man, and together, we gotta figure this shit out. You need to chill for now, though, and take some time again. Come back from this when you're ready."

"Jamir, it's kind of hard to imagine coming back without them. I don't know if I can chill, and if I do, I don't know how long. We gotta get on this quickly. Can't let a muthafucka get away with this shit. That's a violation that I gotta handle. That's my word. That's how I honor the memory—by making the muthafuckas who did this pay."

Jamir heard and felt Danny's pain. He knew all too well how it felt. His sister, Missy, was his everything, and he still wanted revenge for her death. Before Jamir had a chance to respond, he was hit with a busy signal from the other end, informing him that Danny had hung up.

He didn't even have a chance to ask where he was, but if Jamir knew Danny like he thought he did, he already had a clue. Jamir was sure that Danny was somewhere with a female, getting one in, even during his time of mourning. Jamir chuckled and shook his head in disbelief, thinking back to what he had heard on the Evening News.

"Good evening. This is Jessa Trembley with the Channel 7 Crime Alert. The local police responded to an emergency call that came from this house behind me. Once they arrived here, they had to force themselves inside, where they were then welcomed with a scene straight out of a horror film. Inside the house, investigators say that they found a young pregnant woman on the floor with her throat slashed, and her son, who police believed to be around two years old, beside her. The first responders performed an emergency C-section to save the baby inside of her, but it was too late. So far, police have no leads and no motive in this case. Anyone who has any information on this horrible tragedy is asked to reach out to law enforcement. Anything you can give them will help. Thank you for watching Channel 7 News. Back to you, Dave."

Jamir pulled the small piece of paper back out of his pocket and studied it for a minute. He then pulled his cell phone from his other pocket and dialed. As soon as the person on the other end answered, Jamir spoke. "Yeah, go ahead and count me in."

Chapter 7

Denard sat all alone on his newly purchased leather couch, watching his seventy-inch flatscreen as the Baltimore Ravens played against the Arizona Cardinals. Lamar Jackson had been his favorite quarterback ever since he signed for the league. But at that moment, Denard couldn't enjoy the game passes he was throwing.

Ever since his cousin's death, he had been in a zone and hadn't quite figured out how to escape it. Trish had actually been more like a sister to him than anything, and he wasn't sure how to move on without her.

Denard slowly nursed on the warm bottle of Old English 800, his favorite beverage. He waited for the knock, a knock he knew would eventually come. His fo fo lay close by his side just in case he needed it. He hated having to live like that, but he had no other choice. Denard had been stabbed in the back many times by niggas he broke bread with every day, so it had become the norm for his piece to stay loaded and ready. His motto was, 'Stay ready so you ain't got to get ready.'

Denard lifted the bottle to his lips. He heard the knock he had been waiting for. The knock was light, and a normal person might not have heard it, but it was loud enough to get his attention. Denard slowly leaned forward, then set the half-empty bottle on the coffee table. Then he slowly stood up. His six-foot-eight stature should have brought muthafuckas to their knees, but Denard hated violence. He only used it as a last resort. Plus, the last thing he needed was a murder charge lingering over his head.

Without picking up his weapon, Denard walked to his front door and opened it. He could tell that Danny had been crying, but his tears didn't mean shit to him. Denard told Trish time and time again not to fuck with Danny's ass, but there was something about him she couldn't stay away from. Denard felt that if she had listened, she would still be alive. Trish had never done any harm to anybody, so Denard knew her death was something that had to do with Danny. Denard stared deep into Danny's eyes, and as badly as he wanted to snap his neck, he held back. He wanted to see just what this nigga had to say.

"The fuck is you knocking at my door for, man? And don't you say you here the check on me and my well-being, because I personally don't have time for that phony shit right now."

"Come on, Denard. I know you ain't never cared for me, but I had genuine love for your cousin. Man, I know I wasn't right all the time to her, man, but I truly love that girl. And I don't know what I'm gonna do without her and my son. Man, they didn't deserve this. Man, we gotta join forces and find out who did this shit so we can get the muthafuckas."

"No, nigga, you got shit wrong. Ain't no muthafuckin' *we*. I know you ain't give a shit about my cousin. She ain't mean shit to you. If she did, you wouldn't have been slanging your dick all over the hood. Yo' ass should have been at that house with her instead. That should have been your throat them muthafuckas slashed, playa."

"Nard, you don't even know what you're talking about. Trish always liked to make muthafuckas think that I did her so dirty, but if she wouldn't have kept showing her ass, I wouldn't have had to run off with those other bitches. My home should have been my peace, not my headache. You was given the wrong info, bro."

"First of all, I ain't your bro, so miss me with that shit. Second of all, you causing me to miss my game to have me standing here, entertaining your bullshit. I knew you would have eventually shown your face, but I thought that when you did, you would man up and take responsibility for your actions. I know you don't want to carry any of the blame, but my cousin is gone because of you and your drama. When you feel like you're ready to admit that, then you could come back and see me. Maybe then I'll help you figure something out. Until then, nigga, get the fuck on, and you can kiss my black ass."

Denard slammed the door in Danny's face and shook his head. The nerve of that muthafucka to show up at his door and still not own up to his role in Trisha's death. It was ok, though, because one day, Danny would have to answer for everything he'd done.

Then he walked over to his coffee table and picked up his remote control. He was tired of looking at their big asses run back and forth across the field. Besides, the Ravens were behind, and from the way they had been playing, there would be no catching up.

Denard was ready to look at something softer. And he knew just where to go. He picked up his gun from the couch and walked to the bedroom. As soon as he opened the door, he smiled because, honestly, he couldn't help himself.

Denard's girl always had a way of bringing him out of a slump. He licked his lips and looked her up and down as she lay asleep. The vanilla-caramel-complexioned color of her skin was smooth and flawless, and he loved to run his hands all over it. She was the one for him, and no one else dared say something different. He had met her through her cousin a few years back when she moved to town from New Orleans. One look, and Denard knew he had to have her. Not only was she pretty, but she was very smart, and that turned him on more than anything.

Then he walked over to the bed and grabbed his manhood. He leaned over and ran his tongue down her G-string-covered ass crack. That was only a small fraction of what he was ready to do to her. When he traced the length of her leg with his finger, she stirred, and when he sucked her big toe into his mouth, she opened her eyes and turned over to face him.

"Ohh, hey, daddy. I have to admit, that's the best alarm clock in the world—makes a bitch wanna hit snooze just so it can go off over and over again."

"No, baby. This alarm clock ain't got a snooze button, so it won't be no shutting it off. It's programmed to keep on going, ya feel me?"

"No, not yet, daddy, but I can't wait until I do. I'm already wet and ready, just thinking about that dick. What I don't understand is why it ain't inside me yet. Why we still talking?"

"Shit, say less. You ain't said nothing but a word."

Denard got undressed and lowered himself onto the bed beside the woman he would give his life for. He was ready to fuck her real good. All the grief he felt from the death of his cousin, along with all the other bullshit he had been going through would be released through some awesome sex. He knew his girl wouldn't mind, because she liked it when he gave it to her rough, although it wasn't very often.

Denard had always tried to be gentle and make love to her because he never wanted her to feel like she was some kind of trick. Little did he know, she wanted him to make her feel like a whore.

She wanted to tell him, but she didn't want to risk losing him. That was why she found somebody on the side. She just had to make sure that Denard never found out because, if he did, she was sure that he would turn into a-whole-nother person, and she didn't want to meet that one.

After Denard got a good nut and released his seeds deep inside of her, he rolled off her and onto his back. He knew that she had already cum a couple of times, so that left them both satisfied. When she got close and laid her head on his chest, Denard wrapped her in his arms.

He loved to show her as much affection as he could because women loved that type of stuff. Plus, he wanted to make sure she never got it from someone else.

As Denard held her close, he thought about the visit he had just had from Danny and wondered if he had been too harsh on him. He had to remember that, even though the nigga a was a piece of shit to Trish, he was a good father to their son. He knew how bad it hurt to lose his cousin, but he couldn't even begin to imagine how it would feel to lose a child, and hoped he would never, ever find that out.

While his girl fell asleep in his arms, Denard found it hard to close his eyes. He had made up his mind to seek Danny out and apologize for the way that he'd handled him at such a difficult time—not because Denard was a pussy or was soft, but because he had a heart. He just didn't know his was about to be ripped completely out of his chest.

Chapter 8

Jamir had thought about asking Danny to go on a ride with him to meet with Ernesto, but he knew Danny had not been in the right state of mind since losing Trish and his children. He also wasn't sure he wanted Danny in his business like that. Plus, he was given orders to go alone.

Jamir was skeptical at first when asked to make the run, but he didn't think that Jason Barnes was the type of nigga to put him in any bullshit. He just hoped that he was right. Jamir pulled into Arby's parking lot, then drove back around and parked beside a set of dumpsters, like he was told to do. He sat still for a minute, observing his surroundings, before finally stepping out of his ride.

When he walked into the restaurant, nothing but white faces turned to look at him, and it made Jamire feel uneasy. He had heard the rumors that black people didn't eat there, but he didn't believe it until he saw it with his own eyes. Jamir hoped the white people didn't mind eating with a black dude in their presence because he hadn't eaten anything all day and was hungry.

Despite all the people staring at him, Jamir walked up to the counter and was greeted by a white chick with big blue eyes and fiery red hair, and he suddenly found himself missing Rachel. In his mind, he still believed that once he was ready to, he would show the world that she belonged to him.

Raw pulled that slick move and messed it up. Now that Rachel was locked up, and he didn't know when or if he would ever see her face again, he thought maybe things had happened the way that they did because he made the wrong choice by wanting to be with her. That messed with him real bad, but he wasn't about to stand there and dwell on it. He had other stuff to think about, like his growling stomach at this moment.

"How are you doing, sir? Can I help you with something?"

"Uh, yeah. Let me get one of those roast beef sandwiches, uh, with some fries. Matter of fact, go ahead and give me two. I'm hungry as hell."

The cashier giggled when Jamir rubbed his stomach and ordered the extra food. She found him very amusing and decided to flirt. She had never been with a black guy before and wondered if the stories about them were true. She would gladly be a willing participant in testing that theory, so she tried her luck.

"You cute, but I bet you ain't from around here, are you?"

"Nah, this ain't my style. The fuck is all the black people in it though?"

"Ohh, there's a few around. They just don't come here very often. I guess roast beef just ain't their thang. How long are you gonna be around? I mean, I could be an excellent tour guide."

"No, thanks. I ain't looking for no tour or anything like that. Besides, I don't even plan on being here long enough to entertain one. I'm only here on business, and once it's handled, my black ass out."

"Ohh, come on now, cutie. You sure you can't stay and spare a few extra minutes? You never know; I might be able to give you a reason to stay a little longer, or at least one that will keep you coming back."

Jamir shook his head and laughed. He had to give it to her. She was bold, and he kind of liked it, but because he hadn't gone there to hook up, he would have to pass. About to respond and turn her all the way down, a voice came from behind and paused his words.

"You traveled a long way, young man. I know it wasn't so you could fuck the help."

Jamir turned around to the voice and was greeted by a short, bald man. His tan skin was smooth as silk, made like butter. Jamir wondered if he'd had some work done. His deep, Spanish accent held authority. And the diamond-cut Cuban link around his neck screamed *boss*. Little did he know, he wasn't about to run shit Jamir did.

"Who the fuck are you to determine where my dick should go?"

The man lifted his eyebrows as if he were shocked that the young black man spoke to him the way that he did. He expected people to address him with respect, and mostly everyone he encountered did. However, he decided to cut Jamir some slack since he had no clue who he was talking to.

"I'm Ernesto Suarez, and I will let this disrespect go because, at this point, you don't know any better. Now, unless you need something else from this God-awful establishment, we need to be on our way."

"Ohh shit, my bag. Jason didn't tell me what you look like, so my apologies, sir, but you still can't determine where I push my dick."

"Is true, but I'd hate to see you waste it on the low grade of beef, when I have top quality purebreds at my beck and call. Your choice, though."

Jamir turned to look back at the cashier and could tell that Ernesto had hurt her feelings, but it wasn't his place to comfort her. Jamir shrugged his shoulders, threw her the deuces sign, and walked out the door with the man who had ruined her vibe.

Once they walked outside, Jamir turned to go to his ride but noticed that it was no longer where he'd left it. He blinked his eyes a couple of times because he thought he was tripping, but there was no other dumpster in sight in the parking lot. He quickly pulled out his cell phone so he could get to the app that would locate it, but before he had a chance to push any buttons on the screen, Ernesto stopped him.

"You won't be able to find it like that, at least not at this moment. Your tracker was disabled by my people so they could do what they needed to do. I can assure you, though, it is in very good hands and will be returned to you in the same condition you left it in. Now, why don't you come take a ride with me?"

Jamir looked over at the black Escalade that was pulled up beside them, and when the driver's side window went down, he smirked at the person behind the wheel. He reminded Jamir a lot of Brian and hoped he wouldn't have to smoke him. The thought made Jamir feel for his nine, but he realized that he'd left it in his car, a move he hoped he wouldn't regret.

"What's up with you muthafuckas having yo' boys drive you around like you Miss Daisy or something? I don' seen too much of this shit going around."

"Wait 'til you reach the status I'm at. You gon' need one too."

Ernesto smiled and got in his ride, and although he hesitated, Jamir got in behind him. Hell, he didn't seem to have any other choice. No one spoke during the ride, and Jamir made sure to pay close attention to every street sign they passed. He needed to make sure he could send directions just in case things didn't turn out as expected.

He couldn't help it, but his paranoia was on high alert and would stay that way until he pulled back in his own driveway and walked through his front door. Jamir caught the driver cutting his eyes at him several times and suddenly wished that he had turned the job down. It had been his strong desire for the come up that made him go all the way through.

He knew of many men who had lost their lives after being greedy for the almighty dollar. Jamir wasn't trying to lose his life, especially after what that shit with Raw had done to him. He swore to himself if he made it out alive, he would tell Jason Burns to kiss his ass if he ever asked him to go again.

Jamir, sitting there, had been lost in his thoughts when he felt the vehicle come to a complete stop. He couldn't believe he had lost focus and missed the last few turns they made that would have told him where he was. He ensured himself he would not slip like this again.

Jamir shook his head in disappointment and then looked out of the window to see where he had been taken. When he did, he was blinded by the bright lights that surrounded a kingdom. It seemed to be even grander than the one Timbo had lived in with his Russian whore. Jamir sat and admired the palatial estate, and only when he felt a tap on his arm did he break his stare.

"You're going to just sit there and stare? Or are you going to get out and come inside so you can see what your future could hold?"

"Ohh, my bad. I was just in awe right now. This place is tight, and I can already see myself driving up to something like this one day—that is if the enemy don't take my ass out first."

"You shall have this. But you can't let thoughts of being eliminated by the opps be your focus. Now, let's get down to business. Come on, and get up out of this back seat. I'm a little stuffed in here."

Ernesto got out of the car, and Jamir followed suit, but he walked slowly so he could admire the immaculate landscape. When Jamir stopped at the flowing waterfall, Ernesto stood to the side and let him have his moment. Ernesto then pulled the coin from his pocket and passed it to the young street thug.

"Here you go. Throw this one in there and make a wish. If you take it seriously, it just might come true."

Jamir took the coin from Ernesto's hand, and he turned back to look at the water. He then shrugged his shoulders before throwing the coin. Jamir wasn't sure if what he had asked for would really happen, but he was willing to believe it for just a moment.

Jamir and Ernesto made it to the front door, opened it, and a cute Asian girl wearing a mask and uniform appeared. She greeted them with a silver tray that held two drinks. Ernesto reached out and took his, but Jamir shook his head. He smiled at the gesture but turned it down. He wasn't completely comfortable yet, so he had to keep his head clear so he could be ready for anything. The Asian girl winked at him, and when Ernesto placed his empty glass back on the tray, she turned and walked away.

"It's fine for you to relax, young man. No one here is gonna do anything to you, so there will be no drama. It will be kind of hard to enjoy yourself when you're so uptight."

"Nah, I'm cool, just trying to feel out shit, you know? Thought this was going to be an in-and-out thing. I see that it's not. So, uh, yeah, I'm gonna chill."

"I do understand exactly what you mean, but moving one hundred kilos from one spot to another is no easy task. You might as well have some fun while you wait."

Jamir had to think about what Ernesto had just said. True enough, it had been a while since he had some fun for real. Jamir had always taken his business dealings seriously, but he decided that maybe a little excitement wouldn't hurt him.

"I'll tell you what; I'ma chill out and enjoy myself, but there can't be no drugs or alcohol involved for me. I'd like to keep my mind sharp and ready for anything, you understand?"

"Very well. Now come on inside and get comfortable. Got some things in here you're going to like."

Jamir shrugged his shoulders and then followed Ernesto into the rest of the house. The floor-to-ceiling windows held an awesome view of an oval-shaped pool in the backyard, but it was the topless females that caught Jamir's attention.

It seemed that there was every flavor on the menu: chocolate, vanilla, even butter pecan. Jamir rocked up instantly but then remembered that the biggest mistake a corner boy could make was dipping in some strange pussy. None of these bitches belonged to him and never would. He knew that if he messed with any of them, he would have a whole new set of issues, and that was the last thing that he wanted.

"Hey, all this is nice, but I think I'm gonna pass on the pussy. A nigga like me don't need no drama."

"Come on, Jamir. This is the life you want. You might want to go ahead and sample it. My ladies know that there are never any strings attached. Drama is the last thing you need to worry about. Besides, Malcolm would never set you up like this."

"Who the fuck did you just say?"

When Jamir heard Malcolm's name, it burned deep in his soul. He even avoided talking to him for a while, and he was sure that Malcolm would eventually reach out himself as if nothing had happened. But a muthafucka was going to have to straighten Jamir out one way or the other.

"Chill out, young man. I didn't mean to offend you. You should have known that a man in my position would do his homework. I mean, I know Barnes's word is good as gold, but I still needed to check things out for myself. I know that Malcolm has been your go-to for a while, and I don't mean to put him out there like that disrespectfully in his name, but I was just stating facts. I know what his limits are, and I'm sure you do as well."

"Yeah, well, since you did your homework, you should already know that his name tastes like shit in my mouth. That muthafucka did something to me that can't be overlooked. What I'm trying to figure out, though, is what the hell he got to do with anything?"

"Apologies, but you mind me asking what he did to you that would make you feel this way?"

"Ain't shit you need to worry about because what's done is done now. I came here to do a favor for Barnes, and that should be the only thing we need to discuss."

"I respect the fact that you're so bold, and I understand, but I might I say one last thing? Malcolm is not my friend, nor is he my opp. But whatever someone has you thinking he has done to you, that's something you should not believe. Understanding who he is and what he has done, I doubt it. Hearsay gets innocent people killed and blinds you, so that could be avoided if things are investigated properly. Malcolm is a very good businessman, and he would never jeopardize himself for what he has worked for, to cross someone he can depend on and has built so much with. I want you to think about that before you make any rash decisions about your future."

"So that's what you think, huh?"

"No, young blood. That's what I know. Malcolm is a smart man who does good business with everyone he comes across. Even if he unintentionally wrongs you, he will do whatever he can to make it right. That is just how he rolls. True enough, he is my competition, but if I ever lost myself and needed someone to help me get back on my feet, he would be the one I would call. I know he would not turn on me, even if I were his enemy. Malcolm has been a very good and generous person with you, and I hope you are smart enough not to allow others to make you think any different. Perhaps you should look at the one sitting at your right hand. They're usually the ones you trust the most, but honestly, they're the ones you shouldn't. Now, I don't know about you, but I'm going to check out the ladies."

Ernesto walked away, but Jamir stood for minute, wanting to take the time to think about what he said. He had never really taken the time to question Tomeka on what she claimed to have heard. He just took her word for it. She didn't have a reason to lie to him, at least not one he knew about.

Ernesto mentioned Jamir's right hand, but Danny saved him from what Raw had planned. There was no reason to believe Danny crossed him. If he did, why would he have killed Raw? Jamir was confused about the whole situation, but he was determined to find out the real story. He had made up his mind to see Tomeka as soon as he made it back. He needed to know the real story. For the time being, though, he was going to watch the ladies put on the show, one he hoped would take his mind off everything.

Chapter 9

Antoine heard his bedroom door open. He had seen the female out on the block on his way home that night and decided to pick her up. He figured that since he still had a few rocks in his pocket, he might as well use them to get his dick wet.

Antoine was a six-foot-two pretty boy who liked to get his nails manicured and his feet pedicured. His smooth, light skin and dark-green eyes made it hard for the ladies to resist him, so he never lacked in the pussy department. Everywhere he went, the females would be in awe and throw themselves at him. Antoine had fucked all types of bitches, but the one thing he never had was a crackhead.

Antoine sat around many nights and listened to his boys talk about the many things a fiend would do for a piece of rock. Their talks had intrigued him, but he wasn't satisfied with their words alone. Antoine decided to experience it for himself. He couldn't wait to tell his crew how the hoe had sucked him from his head to his toe, dick to the crack. Her pussy was nice and tight too, and had made it all worth it.

"I'm gonna let you keep fuckin' that hoe, player. All I wanna know is where the stash is at. And don't act like you don't know what I'm talking about. What you decide will determine your fate."

Antoine had been on the verge of getting his nut when he heard the voice come from behind him. The gun cocked, and his dick went limp and slid out of the wetness he had been submerged in. Antoine quickly held his hands up and surrendered, but he wondered why the bitch that lay under him was calm. Most females would have screamed and tried to cover themselves, but not her. Antoine found it strange, which made him extra paranoid.

"Hold up. The fuck is going on here? This supposed to be some kind of setup, bitch? Why are you so calm? You better not let me find out you had a hand in this."

"No. I swear on everything that I love. I didn't know anything about this. You gotta believe me."

The female suddenly became scared and slid out from under Antoine. She then covered herself with the sheet. She could have sworn that she recognized the voice, but she couldn't be one hundred percent sure. And even if she did realize who it was, she knew better than to speak on it. She had a daughter at home, and she couldn't afford to risk that. She quickly regretted getting into Antoine's car and wished she could take it all back, but it was too late for that; all she could do was pray that things turned out in her favor.

Fuck Antoine. She didn't really know his light-skinned ass anyway and couldn't care less about what happened to him. She thought the best thing for her to do was to stay quiet and mind her business, but as soon as she caught the masked man eyeing her, she switched up.

"The hell is you waiting on? Tell that muthafucka what he wants to know so he can take his ass somewhere else. I don't know about you, but I'm not trying to die tonight."

The gunman nodded his head in agreement with what she said. "Yeah, nigga. You might wanna listen to that bitch and save the both of you. I ain't come in here to kill nobody. But if you play hard and don't give me what I want, my plans might just change."

Antoine looked from the female to the man who stood there with his gun pointed at his chest. All Antoine wanted that night was pussy. He never expected to get jacked. That was why he put his gun away. He never thought he would need it for a booty call. He swore to himself, if he made it out of this alive, he would keep his weapon close from that point on, even when he had to take a shit. Antoine let out a long sigh and decided to just cooperate. Whatever he lost would eventually be regained, but he could never get his life back.

"Alright, damn. Let me just throw on some boxers, and I'll show you where it's at."

"Ohh, yeah, you must think I'm a dumb muthafucka to think that I'm gonna let you pull that shit on me. Just tell me where it's at. I don't need you to show me shit."

"I have to show you because you ain't gonna be able to get to it without me. You need my fingerprint."

The gunman stood there and thought about it for a second. He wasn't sure if Antoine was telling the truth, but if he was, he definitely didn't want to miss out on the come-up. After all, that was what he went there for. He knew that Antoine would be an easy target because he lived alone. He never expected the bitch to be there, too. But it was what it was, and if it turned out to be bullshit, he was going to blow Antoine's nut sack right off.

"Ok, I'm gonna let you go ahead and lead me to where it's at, but if you're going on with your dick swingin'—if you make one wrong move, I'm gonna make sure you never make a baby again. You understand me?"

"Yeah, yeah, I got what you're saying, but you ain't even gotta worry about me. I ain't gonna do or try nothing stupid. My question is, what about her? You expect her to sit here and chill while I walk on eggshells with a gun to my back?" Antoine asked, pointing to the female whose eyes grew big as saucers.

She had hoped they would walk out and forget about her even being there. She had already planned to run as soon as they got where they were going, but Antoine and his big-ass mouth messed that all up.

"Ohh, so you thought I forgot about this bitch? Nah. Now, why don't you go ahead and pull that sheet from her and use it to tie her up? Make sure it's tight so she can't get loose. She looks like the type who would try some stupid sheep. Go on ahead and handle that for me so you and I can get down to business."

When the female heard what he said, she held on to the sheet a little tighter, but she was no match against Antoine's strength. He reached over and yanked it from her. He tore the sheet in two and then reached out for her. At first, she tried to pull back, but as soon as she felt the cold steel against her flesh, she surrendered to the gun. They pointed it at her until she was secured to the bedpost, and then she was left alone while Antoine and the jack boy left the room.

That's when Antoine led the way down the hall to a closet door. He stopped and opened it slowly, and then he pushed the clothes hanging in it to the side. He reached out and placed his two thumbs over a small blank square, and five seconds later, the wall slid open, so he led the gunman in and stepped to the side.

"There's the stairs. Take all of it; I don't care. My life is more important than any amount of money or drugs."

"I'm glad you think so. Now, pack these two bags up for me. Make sure they're filled to the top."

The gunman threw two duffel bags at Antoine and watched him fill them up. When they were packed, he took them and threw them across his shoulders and then aimed the gun at Antoine. He fired and put one slug through each of his knees and then turned around and walked out.

Antoine fell to the floor in pain, but somehow, he found the strength to drag himself back to the bedroom. As soon as he made it through the door, the female saw him and gasped. She was grateful that he was alive, so grateful that it jogged her memory.

"Don't worry, Antoine. I know exactly who he was, and I'm gonna lead you straight to him."

Chapter 10

Cassie sat in the corner booth and nursed a Long-Island-Iced Tea while she bobbed her head to the sounds of Rich Homie Quan. She still found it hard to believe that he had died so suddenly and at such a young age. Plies was her favorite rapper, but Rich Homie Quan was second, and even though she never met him personally, she still felt the loss of him as if she had.

"Ohh, bitch, snap out of it. Your mind is supposed to be here with us, not somewhere else. Shit, we've been sitting here trying to get your attention for about five minutes now. What's really up with that?"

Syleena had put her thumb and middle finger together and snapped them in Cassie's face, but she and Chanel could tell her mind was elsewhere. They were pissed because they had all agreed to meet there so they could have a good time. Cassie was ruining everything, though, because it was clear that she wasn't feeling it.

"Hoe, I am not stuntin' either you. I was thinking about Rich Homie Quan's fine ass. I still can't believe he's gone, and I didn't even get a chance to meet him first."

"It wouldn't have mattered if you did, because that man of yours wouldn't have let you enjoy it. That nigga be on your ass for real. I'm shocked he even allowed you to come and hang out with us tonight."

"Fuck you, Syleena, wit' yo' hating ass. Contrary to what you believe, my man don't run shit when it comes to me. He

71

allows me to be my own woman without any rules or boundaries."

"That's what your mouth say, but I can guarantee that if you step out of line, he is gonna get in that ass. Now, tell me it ain't so."

Cassie could only roll her eyes at the comment because what Syleena said was true. Her man was psychotic when it came to her and tried as hard as he could to keep her on a short leash. The only time she could get away would be when he went out of town on a run, which wasn't very often.

When she had run into Danny and spent the two nights in his arms, her man had been on a two-day trip to Brooklyn. If he ever found out she spent those days with the next nigga, he would've killed them both, and since Cassie had fucked up and caught feelings, she knew she would have to keep shit on the low. However, as soon as she heard her girls bring up his name, everything changed.

Chanel tapped Syleena on the shoulder, and as usual, the gossiping began. Chanel stayed in people's business. Anyone who wanted to be in the know about anything could go to her and get all the information they wanted. Nine times out of ten, Chanel and her four-one-one was legit. Her mouth had no filter and held no discrimination. Everyone was in the line of fire and could fall victim to her stories. She didn't care who you were.

"Bitch, did you hear about Trish ghetto ass? The word is, she was split from Eddie, and blood was everywhere. Her little boy, too. By the way, that was foul as hell. He was just a baby and ain't never did nothing to nobody. Only crazy niggas would hurt a child."

"Yeah, girl, I heard about that. But what about the baby she was carrying? It didn't even get to experience one day of life before it was wiped away. I heard she was having a girl. I bet that would have been one pretty baby."

"Pretty? Bitch, not with Danny's one-minute ass as her father. I don't know why Trish stayed with him as long as she did. She should have left him and found some dick that was worth her time. Shit that tired ass nigga already getting his nut before you had time to get your pussy wet to even feel the dick. What type of shit is that?"

"Now, how the hell you know what his dick can do? You talking like you done had it."

"I ain't gonna lie on my pussy, and you know that my dumb ass tried to give him a little. A little was really all I got. Nice, long dildo and these fingers would have done me more justice. Shit, a bitch can count to two, and he's already done."

Chanel and Syleena laughed at Danny's expense, but as soon as they realized Cassie wasn't laughing with them, they stopped. They were used to her joining in and enjoying the gossip sessions. Clearly, she wasn't with it, and they found that off, but Chanel was determined to find out why.

"Uhn-uhn, bitch, why are you sitting there looking crazy? It ain't like we were sitting here talking about yo' man. What's really up with you anyway? You've been acting standoffish all night. Your period on or something?"

"Hell nah. You know I don't come out when my period is on. That's so disgusting to be out in the club with a tampon stuck in your pussy. I ain't been acting no kind of way. I'm just wondering when the hell you fucked Danny. You ain't never mentioned that before."

Syleena gave Cassie a crazy look because she found it strange that she had questioned Chanel about Danny. It was as if she was getting some straightening done. Cassie had a damn good man at home, so Syleena was curious as to why her attitude changed when Danny became the subject. And she knew there was only one way to find out.

"Damn, Cassie. You acting like you offended or something? Is there something going on with you and Danny that you're not telling us? Come on. Spill the beans, bitch."

"Ain't shit up with me and him; we just cool. That's all."

"Ohh yeah, cool. How cool? Is it a homeboy or homegirl type of thing? Or cooler than, 'baby fuck me harder.'?"

"You know what? I don't have to answer to you bitches. My personal life is not your business. I really don't have time for this anyway, so you two can just kiss my ass. I'm out of here." Cassie grabbed her bag and stood up with an attitude. She had had enough of her friends for one night. They were asking way too many questions she didn't want to answer.

Plus, Chanel talked too damn much, and Cassie didn't want to give her anything else to gossip about. However, before she had a chance to step away from the table, Chanel said something that stopped her in her tracks.

"Hum, speak of the devil, and his black ass will appear."

Cassie and Syleena both looked up at the same time and saw Danny entering the club. When Cassie saw that he was by himself, it gave her an instant sense of relief because she wasn't sure how she would have acted had he walked in with another bitch on his side. Thankfully, she didn't have to react to the situation. Without saying a word, she sat back down so she could watch him from a distance, but her eyes weren't on him for long before he noticed her.

Syleena made sure she knew it. "Bitch, his ass coming this way. But I guess since you two are so cool, you ain't got nothing to be worried about, right?"

"No, Syleena. I'm not worried. It's not like that with us."

No sooner than Cassie said it, Danny was in front of her. She didn't know how he had heard her comment over the loud music that was playing, but clearly, he did.

"It ain't like that with who? And why the hell ain't you answering your phone? I was trying to call yo ass for hours."

Selena and Chanel tuned all the way in so they could listen to the exchange between Cassie and Danny—Syleena just because she was so nosy, but Chanel needed a juicy story to talk about. She couldn't wait to put the word out that there, and she knew how others would react to it, especially Cassie's man, whom Chanel had been wanting to fuck for a while. She hoped she would finally get the chance once he found out about Cassie's infidelities.

"My phone was turned off, which is the norm when I'm out with my girls. Was there something you needed?"

"Yeah, I need you to come with me. Get your bag, and let's go."

Cassie hesitated and looked nervously at Chanel and Syleena. She knew that if she got up and left the club with Danny, everyone would hear about it, including her man. As bad as she wanted to jump up and go, she would have to turn him down. However, Danny wasn't going for that. "Look, Danny, I'm chilling with my girls. Besides, who are you to come up in here and demand that I leave with you?"

Then he scratched his eyebrow and thought about what she just said. The nerve of her to diss him in front of anybody pissed him off. He wondered what the hell she was tripping for. They hadn't had an argument, and he felt like he should remind her of that.

"Ohh, so all that talk about playing your position wasn't shit? Because it looks like you just threw a foul ball, but I guess what you won't do, the next bitch will. Now, I'm gonna tell you one more time; get your shit, and let's go."

Syleena and Chanel's eyes grew big as they sat and waited to see what Cassie was going to do. Clearly, there was more going on than she wanted to admit, but she was about to be cold-busted.

Cassie pressed her glossed lips together and grabbed her bag. She then stood and smiled a fake smile at her girls and then stepped away from the table. As soon as Cassie and Danny walked out of the club, Chanel reached for her phone. She couldn't wait to break up a happy home just so she could move in.

Chapter 11

Jamir drove home and tried to remember how many times the bitch that Ernesto had hooked him up with made had him cum. It was just a lot. He would never forget how good she sucked his dick. The bitch was a beast in the bedroom. Jamir had to admit, Ernesto was living the dream. He had plenty of money, a nice crib, and foreign luxury cars in his garage. He had pussy at his disposal, and it wasn't just any type of pussy. It was top of the line.

Ernesto had the top-of-the-line pussy, and Jamir could see himself in his shoes one day. He was glad that he had made the trip. Although at first, he was skeptical, Jamir told himself that he would make sure Jason Barnes knew just how much he appreciated this opportunity.

When Jamir rounded the corner to his house, he saw the county jail and slowed to a stop. His thoughts immediately turned to Rachel. He wondered how she was doing in there and if she had everything she needed. The times they had spent together were deeply ingrained in his mind, and it made him miss her. Jamir knew it was a bad move, but he ached to see her. He felt like it had been forever since he looked into those big, green eyes. They always seemed to hold him captive, and he couldn't help but wonder if they were still the same.

"Fuck it. I gotta do it." Jamir told himself that if he couldn't just pass by and keep it moving, even though he knew it would have been the best thing for him to do, he knew that Rachel didn't have anyone else. He wanted to step up and do the right thing.

Jamir pulled into the parking spot and got out. The average nigga would have worried about the drug stash in his ride, but not Jamir, because his ride had never been hot. Plus, not even a canine could have sniffed out the load that he was carrying. They were hidden too well.

Jamir walked into the jailhouse and took a deep breath. He was nervous, but not because of what he left behind. It was because of whom he was about to face. It had been a minute, and his heart beat fast in anticipation. He had so much he needed to get off his chest and heart. And even though his moment had come, he wasn't sure if he could do it.

When Rachel appeared on the other side of the glass, Jamir wanted to pull her into his arms. However, the barrier between them stopped his approach. His nervousness went away, but anxiety filled its spot. His dick swelled, but it would not find any pleasure, because its desire wasn't within reach. She was close, yet still so far away. As soon as Rachel sat down, Jamir told her just how he felt.

"'Sup, Rachel? I know you're probably finding it hard to believe that I'm in front of you right now, but it's been a minute. I have been missing you. I had to come see you because wasn't no way I could have went another minute."

"Well, Jamir, you might as well get used to it because they're going. They're talking about giving me five years. That's a long time, but I'm sure you will survive because at least you won't have to worry about being seen with me anymore. Plus, you and Erica can live happily ever after with your kid now. Don't that sound right? "

"Five years? You can't be serious? How I'm gonna go that long without feeling you? And Erica? It ain't shit between us but our daughter, and you know that."

"Oh, yeah. A daughter that you and I should have had, but instead of standing up for me, you let that bitch attack my character, and then you rewarded her by giving her a child. So, don't worry, Jamir. I'm sure these next five years will go real smooth for you."

"Come on, Rachel. Give me a fucking break. You act like that shit with Erica was planned or some shit. If I could go back and change things, I would."

"It's too late to change things, Jamir. Lucky for you, I'll be out of your way, and you won't have to worry about me anymore. How many men I fuck before I knock down your door or get in your ride, by the time I get out, you won't even care anymore anyway."

Rachel's words stabbed Jamir deep in his chest. He knew that he hadn't done right by her, but he was there, trying to make it up to her. He couldn't imagine his life without her somewhere in it. Five years would seem like a century when someone cared.

Jamir hated the fact that she was playing hard, but she had every right. Rachel was a woman scorned, scarred by the reality of the shame he felt by loving her. He had broken her, and he only hoped that he could fix it.

"So, I guess I deserve that, but how long you gonna hold it against me? The shit is done and over with. Why you can't move past it, Rachel?"

"Love you, Jamir, more than all the drugs in the world, but every time I was with you, I was reminded that I was just a crackhead. You made sure that all I ever really wanted was you. But maybe I need to start putting my focus elsewhere— take care of myself and be careful out there. I gotta go, but you will always be in my heart, Jamir. Always."

Rachel stood slowly from the hard metal stool she'd been sitting on. She put two fingers to her lips, and as she stared at Jamir deep in his eyes, she pulled those same fingers back and pressed them to the glass that separated her from the man she loved. It would be her final kiss to him. At least that was what she told herself. She needed to let him go and hoped the time she had there would make it easier.

Rachel finally turned and walked away. Once she was out of sight, Jamir sat there alone. He waited and hoped she would change her mind and come back. After a few minutes had passed, he knew she was gone for good. He was hurt beyond health. Suddenly, he felt a tear roll down his cheek, and he wiped it away. Even from behind the walls, she still had control of his emotions, but he knew he had to get it together.

Jamir wiped another tear away and stood up. When he got to the exit door, he looked back one more time to make sure, but she had not returned. Jamir shrugged his shoulders and walked out. As soon as he got into his ride, his cell phone rang. He was so lost in his emotions that he didn't bother to check the caller ID. His mind told him that it was her calling to apologize and ask him to please come back. When he heard the voice on the other end, a different emotion kicked in. *Anger.*

"What's up, Jamir? Why the hell I ain't heard from you in a while? Don't try to feed me no lying or bullshit either. Just give it to me straight."

"Nigga, who? You already know what's up. Don't play with me like I'm a dumb muthafucka."

"Yo, you could stop with that little boy shit. Grow the fuck up and tell me what the hell is going on."

"What's going on, is that shit you plotted on me right with Raw. I forgave you for sticking your dick to my bitch because of your ignorance, but yeah, that last game you and that bitch ass hoe Raw pulled on me? It's something I ain't gonna never let go. Muthafucka, you gonna have to answer for that move."

"The fuck is you talking about, playa'? I ain't never plotted a damn thing against you. Someone put some bullshit in your ear, but you had better clean it real quick. You need to know you talking facts before you speak about it, and before you make an idle threat against me, just know that shit can go both ways."

"So what you saying, bro? We can go ahead and meet up somewhere and handle this like two grown muthafuckas? Ain't no need for all this rattling off over the phone shit. A nigga like me stay ready, and I ain't never scared."

"Then name the time and place, and I'll be there early."

"Bet that."

Jamir knew he didn't have to meet up with Jason Barnes until the following day, so he gave Malcolm instructions on where they needed to meet up right then and disconnected the phone. He threw this phone in the passenger seat and started his ride.

Jamir already had so much anger built up inside from all the shit that had been happening in his life. He was too young to have gone through so much, but as he thought about it, the rage continued to build. The first thing that came to his mind was how his own mother had left him and Missy for a man. What kind of woman could do that to the children she gave life to? He wondered if she ever regretted her decision or even thought about them. Missy's death suddenly filled his mind. It shattered him into pieces, and there was no glue strong enough to put them back together. Many days, he woke up and wanted to join her, but first, he had to avenge her.

Jamir's connect had fucked the woman he loved and plotted to take all he had worked so hard for. At least that's what he had been told. And just when he didn't think things could get any worse, the one woman who could bring him to his knees was out of his reach and wanted nothing else to do with him. Even the daughter he loved so much was out of his reach. That one night with a bitch he could no longer stand to be around turned into a trap. There was nothing he could do about it because the seed had been planted and left him with an eighteen-year obligation.

Jamir had gotten to the point that he felt he had no one, not even the nigga that rode beside him. He wanted to be able to trust Danny, but he just couldn't shake the feeling inside of him. He couldn't afford to take any more chances but hoped one day Danny would erase whatever doubts he had. Even though he claimed to have saved him from Raw's intentions, Jamir still had the feeling that he didn't. There was nothing he could do to change it.

Jamir pushed past the thoughts in his mind and pulled into the apartment complex he had told Malcolm to meet him at. He looked around, but as far as he could tell, Malcolm hadn't made it yet. Jamir pulled out his gun and made sure it was loaded and ready, just in case something unexpected popped off or rubbed him the wrong way. His well-being had already been threatened once, and although he pulled through, he couldn't be so sure he'd be lucky the next time. Jamir had so many reasons to live and stay safe, and avenging his sister's murder was number one. Everything else on his agenda wasn't as pressing. Missy deserved justice, and Jamir was determined to get it.

Jamir finally got out of his car and looked around again. The complex was quiet and seemed deserted, which seemed strange to him because there were usually a few niggas out and pulling in those last-minute pennies, just like he used to do. He still remembered those days when he needed those pennies just to make ends meet.

Jamir respected the niggas that put in work and got it from the grind instead of pulling jack moves on the next man. Those were the kind of thugs he liked to work with, but they also came few and far between. He had thought Raw was one of them, but he'd been wrong. It wasn't for him to worry about, though, because he learned his lesson, and he vowed never to do the recruiting thing again.

Once he finally felt comfortable enough, he walked up to the apartment, the one he told Malcolm to meet him in, and knocked. He was glad he had beaten Malcolm there because it gave him some time to ask questions of his own. He hoped the bitch had told him the truth the first time, because he'd hate to be made a fool of.

He stood and stared at the door, wondering what could be taking so long. Finally, he knocked again. He heard a whirring sound come from the other side, and then the door opened.

"Dayum. What the fuck happened to you? Last time I was here, you ain't look like that." Tomeka rolled her eyes, then pushed the button that backed her wheelchair up. Jamir looked down and noticed that both of her legs were in casts. He wondered if something had gone down with her and Danny after he'd left. He knew this boy had done some crazy things, but what he saw was pushing the limit. Jamir shook his head and closed the door behind him, and then he followed Tomeka to the living room.

"Don't worry, Jamir. I know what you're thinking, but it wasn't Danny who did this to me."

"Ohh yeah? Well, what happened then? You fell down some stairs or something?"

"I wish that. These two broken ankles are courtesy of Blount's black ass. He came back here and wanted to know exactly what happened to that bitch he called a partner. I tried to play stupid, but when he snapped the first ankle, my ass loosened up. I talked and told him almost everything."

"Man, that's foul. So why he snapped the other one? And what exactly did you tell him?"

"He snapped the other one to make sure I didn't go nowhere, just in case he had to come back and get some more information. Ohh, this hurts."

"Ok, but you didn't answer my other question. What did you tell that muthafucka?"

Tomeka got quiet and looked away. She wondered how Jamir would react if she told him that she had thrown Danny under the gun, and because of that, Trish and her children had been killed. She hadn't verified it yet, but she could feel it. They were sure Blount was the one who had them murdered. She wasn't even sure that she wanted to know the truth because the thought of that alone made her sick to her stomach. She knew Jamir wanted answers so he would know what to expect, but before Tomeka could say another word, a knock sounded at her door.

Jamir saw her jerk in fear and reassured her. "Just chill. They're here for me."

Jamir made sure his gun was accessible before he opened the door. He wasn't sure what frame of mind Malcolm would be in, so he needed to be prepared for anything. Jamir opened the door and looked Malcolm in the eyes. Ever since that nigga fucked Rachel, things hadn't been the same between them. Jamir hated that, and it went so far, and it felt like there was no going back. He would do whatever he had to do to protect himself, even killing Malcolm if it came down to that.

Malcolm held his arms up, just in case Jamir wanted to pat him down. He didn't know what his young protege's problem was, but what he needed him to know was that he'd come in peace. When Jamir shook his head, Malcolm dropped his arms, shrugged his shoulders, and then walked in. When Jamir shut the door behind him, Malcolm turned around so they could face each other once again. He didn't have time for bullshit, so he got right down it.

"A'ight, bro. We're here now, face to face. Now what? You want to tell me what the hell is going on with you?"

"Don't worry. We're gonna get down to all of that. But first, I got someone I think you should meet."

"Ok, lead the way."

"Nah, nigga. This is how shit gon' work. I'ma gonna give you the directions, and you gonna do the honors. Now, turn around, and walk straight down the hallway."

Malcolm shook his head and turned around. He wasn't worried about having his back to Jamir because Jamir had never been the type of dude who would pull a sneak attack from behind. He would rather look a muthafucka in their eyes and handle business that way.

Malcolm was still confused about when and why shit had gotten so bad between them. He thought Jamir had gotten over the mistake of him messing around with Rachel, but it was obvious that he was still holding a grudge.

Malcolm walked slowly and steadily down the short hallway until he entered the living room. He noticed the female in the wheelchair and wondered what had happened to her. His first thought was that Jamir had done something to this young lady because both of her lower legs were in casts, but he wasn't sure what role she played in everything.

"Go ahead and sit down. The lady right here has a lot to say, and I don't want you to miss not one word."

Malcolm sat down in the chair across from the female, while Jamir stood up. Malcolm had already made peace with his creator, just in case things turned sour, but he'd hoped it wasn't going to come to that. He finally focused on her, but she acted like she didn't know what was going on either. Thankfully, Jamir reminded her.

"Ohh yeah. I forgot to introduce the two of you. Tomeka, this man right here—this is Malcolm."

Tomeka's eyes grew big, as if she had seen a ghost. She looked at Malcolm and then at Jamir but said nothing. She knew that she had gotten caught in her lies and had no way out of them—unless, of course, she told the real truth.

Chapter 12

Cassie bit down hard on her bottom lip. She was on the verge of getting a good, much-needed orgasm, and she was ready for it. All of a sudden, Danny stopped what he had been doing. Cassie opened her eyes and looked down at him like he'd lost his mind. The shit he pulled would have been typical for a selfish nigga who only cared about their own needs, but he had never struck her as such.

"Damn it, Danny! Why the hell did you stop? That tongue was feeling so good to me, and I was just about to cum."

"Ohh yeah? Well, right before I was about to give you that good ass nut, my mind went somewhere else. So, you want to make me understand why you had your cell phone turned off? Anything other than that is irrelevant."

"Oh my gosh, really? I can't believe you're still on that when I already told you that I like to turn it off when I'm out with my girls. Them some nosy ass hoes, and I don't want them in my business like that. What is the big deal anyway? Hell, I thought you'd be shut in somewhere, still mourning your losses."

"Don't get cute. Besides, you're the one who said you could play your position without any drama. But it seems to me that you eating those words. It sounds like you hating on the bitch that ain't even around no more."

"I ain't hating. But since you want to bring up my position, shouldn't I be up for promotion since the numero uno bitch is gone?"

"Careful how you speak 'cause you're making a nigga feel real paranoid right now. You sure you ain't had something to do with getting her out of the picture just so you could step up?"

"You know better than that."

"Do I? Shit, I only been messing with you for a hot second now. I don't know what you're capable of."

"Oh, now stop playing. I'm not capable of taking someone's life. I mean, I know I talk a lot of stuff, and I'm glad that that bitch is out of the way, but I would never wish anything like that on nobody. Oh my God, especially a child. I can't even begin to imagine what you're going through."

Danny knew that Cassie was telling the truth, but he needed to find someone besides himself to blame. He had been wronged by a lot of muthafuckas that would have loved to get at him, but he never thought any of them would have been cruel enough to harm a child or even his girl while she was carrying another.

He and Trish had been through a lot of shit, but he never would have wished death on her. He knew eventually, word of who'd done it would get out, and when it did, he would get Trish and his children the justice they deserved. Until then, he would continue to live his life as if nothing had ever happened.

"Look, I'm sorry. I'm just tripping right now. My head is in a lot of places, so don't take anything I say too personal. However, make sure, from this day on, you keep your phone on at all times. A nigga might need you when you least expect it."

"Ok, that was my bad. It won't happen again. Now can't you finish what you started?"

Danny smiled and spread Cassie's legs so he could dive back in, but before his mouth made contact with her womanhood, his cell phone vibrated. He looked at Cassie, who, in turn, shook her head. He had a good mind to ignore the call, but since he knew it wasn't Trish, he decided to answer it.

Cassie sat up on the bed and pouted while Danny walked into the seating area of the room. She felt like the only reason he wouldn't talk in front of her was because some bitch was on the other end of this call. She knew Danny had messed around with a lot of women before her, but she felt like she didn't deserve the disrespect. Trish was out of the way, and the last thing she wanted to do was compete with someone else. She had even thought about breaking up with her man just so she could be all the way with Danny. Thankfully, she hadn't made that move yet. Danny finally walked back into the room while Cassie was getting dressed.

"The fuck is you doing? I ain't done with you yet."

"Well, I'm done with you. And to think I was gonna leave my man for you."

"Yo' man? You ain't tell me you had a man."

"Would it have really mattered if I did?"

"Ohh. No, I was gonna get in that pussy whenever I wanted regardless."

"Keep dreaming, nigga. My ass is out." Cassie picked up her bag and walked out. Danny didn't try to stop her, because he knew she would be back.

Chapter 13

Jamir sat in the darkness of the night and waited for Jason Barnes to show up so he could pass off what belonged to him. Jamir hadn't touched anything and wasn't going to without Barnes being present. He didn't even pull out the twenty-five keys he was promised for doing the run.

He just wanted to make sure there was no misunderstanding. Jamir wanted to keep shit between them so he didn't jeopardize any future dealings. Jamir was agitated, though, and was clearly ready to get things over with because he had bigger issues to deal with. He was also still trying to process that Tomeka had told him the truth to begin with. And what she had gained from it? Shit seemed crazy to him, but he'd already seen it coming.

The brightness of the lights brought him out of his thoughts, and he quickly reached over and unlocked the passenger side door. When Barnes got in, he could tell from the look on Jamir's face that he had a lot going on, which made him wonder if he already knew about what had happened. But he wanted to handle business first and find out exactly what Jamir knew.

"'Sup, man? 'Cause why you looking like you somewhere else right now? You wanna tell me about it?"

"No, I'm good, bro. And what I got going on ain't got nothing to do with what's going on with us right now. Between us is sweet, so let's keep it that way."

"Yeah, so that means everything went right?"

"Everything went as you said it would, except for a couple of small surprises along the way, though."

Barnes already knew Jamir was talking about Ernesto's women. He had his own dick sucked a few times, but he always refused to have sex with them. He didn't trust females he knew nothing about and refused to take a chance. He didn't have to. Barnes was glad Jamir enjoyed himself. He just hoped he'd never regret it.

"Ok, that's what's up. I'm glad you could get away and enjoy yourself. Ernesto has a fine stable of women, but tread lightly. I would hate to see you get hemmed up by one of them, if you know what I mean."

"Ohh, you ain't gotta worry about that. A bitch can't hem me up if I don't let them. Now, let's go ahead on and unload what's yours, and I got some other shit I need to handle."

"I hope your boy Danny is included in what you got to handle 'cause word on the street is he pulled the jack move on one of mine."

"Hold up, bro. Who told you about some shit like that?"

"What do you mean? I really ain't wanna be the one to tell you, but I don't have any other choice. It was your baby mama who had put his name out there. She just happened to be with Antoine when it all went down. Supposedly, that nigga was masked up, but she recognized his voice."

"The fuck was Erica doing with a nigga in your set? Was my fucking daughter there too?"

"Look, man. It ain't my job to keep tabs on nobody's bitch, but I ain't sliding with you. All I know is what she said. It was your boy. I didn't want to make any moves without talking to you first, since that's your people and all. But if that nigga runs up in any other place that my people chill in, I'm gonna make a cold move. And when I do? Everyone gon' freeze. You get what I'm saying?"

"Yeah, I definitely get *exactly* what you're saying. But I don't control shit that nigga does, so watch how you move. I ain't got no beef with you, and I ain't trying to start nothing either. My boy or not, keep me out of it. I'll get up with him and give him the word. But if he don't listen, that's on him and him alone."

"That's cool as long as you and me on the same page. Now, let's handle what we met up for."

Jamir gave Barnes the cocaine he owed him and then drove away with his own. The twenty-five keys had been an easy come-up, but it wasn't one he wanted all the time. Jamir had his own stash and didn't think it was a good idea to be sitting on too much. He knew it was time to hit the streets and push what he could, but first, he had to make another stop.

As soon as Erica opened her apartment door, Jamir put his hand around her neck and pushed her back against the wall. She grabbed his arm to try to pull it down, but her strength couldn't match his, so she finally just submitted. She didn't think he would go all the way to kill her, so why put up a fight and waste her energy?

"Bitch, where the fuck was my daughter at when you had that next nigga sticking dick to you?"

Jamir saw that Erica was having a hard time answering him, so he released her from his grip. He was pissed but didn't realize he had such a tight hold onto her. In his mind, he wanted to kill that bitch, but his heart wouldn't let him—not because he gave a damn about her or had any real feelings for her. He would let her keep living for his daughter's sake. Jamir knew he was in no position to raise a little girl, so Erica had been spared for that reason.

"Really, nigga? Where do you think she was at, huh? You think I had her sitting in her highchair next to the bed or some shit so she could watch? Can't you give me a little bit of credit? I'm a good mutha to her, and you know it. I would never go somewhere to freak off like that with her on my hip. I don't have to respect you, but I gave her life, and I owe it to her."

"You do owe her respect, but you're gonna show me some too, whether you want to or not."

"Jamir, fuck you! I don't gotta show you shit. Now, if you'll excuse me, I need to go pick our daughter up from my auntie's house."

"The hell is she doing over there?"

"Ohh, come on now. Don't all of a sudden question me about why she is somewhere else. It ain't like you come over here and see her every day. Hell, to be honest, you ain't been over here in a minute."

Jamir felt the jab as soon as Erica said those words. He had to admit, he hadn't been that great of a dad to his daughter. Jamir felt if he made sure she had what she needed, that was all that mattered. He rarely went to Erica's to see his little girl, mainly because he was always too busy, and with the street shit, he never thought about how his absence would affect anyone else.

"Look, you're right. I'm gonna work on that. I just be trying to handle my business, and it takes up a lot of my time."

"Well then, don't get mad when that time comes from someone else. You gotta remember that I got a life too. I'm still young like you, and I have needs, so when you don't show up to take her and spend time with her, I take her where she's safe."

"You got needs, huh? So, you and Antoine are a thing now?"

"Me and Antoine ain't shit, but he's good to have around when the girl gets wet. You ain't putting in no work no more, so somebody's gonna do it."

"Yeah, well, they can keep on doing it, too. I need you to know what happened, though. Someone told me you dropped Danny's name."

Erica rolled her eyes and crossed her arms over her chest before letting out a long sigh. She really didn't feel like telling the same story over and over again, but she knew that

Jamir wouldn't leave until he got the information he wanted out of her.

"So, what if I did? That bastard busted in and messed up my whole group. His coward ass wouldn't even show his face, but I recognized his voice, though it took me a little minute to catch it. But it was him. I know he recognized me too, and he probably couldn't wait to tell you I was fucking Antoine."

"Just so you know, Danny wasn't the one who ratted you out. However, in the future, if you lay up with strange niggas from the other side of the block, keep your damn mouth shut when shit like that goes down. I don't give a damn if you know who it is or not. That's why I don't allow you in my business now. Go get my daughter and bring her home. And don't you take your ass back out after that."

Jamir turned and walked out, leaving Erica standing there with an attitude. She couldn't believe he had the audacity to check her on the next nigga. He no longer had that right. The only thing Erica had that he had any reign over was the child that the two of them shared. Everything else was hers. She almost regretted ratting Danny out—almost. But he was a piece of shit to her, and whatever happened to him would be well-deserved.

When Jamir got back in his ride, he sat there for a minute, wondering how often Erica passed his little girl off to someone else.

The thought alone had him wanting to choke that bitch, but the last thing he needed was for her to leave his daughter without a mother, so he pushed that thought to the side for now.

As soon as Jamir started his car and put it in reverse, his cell phone rang. To be honest, he wasn't in the mood for talking, but he answered it anyway.

"'Sup? This better be good 'cause I got shit to do, so make what you have to say short."

"Damn it, nigga! It's like that? I heard you was looking for me."

Hearing Danny's voice on the other end infuriated Jamir. That nigga stayed in some bullshit, but now he had hit too close for comfort. Jamir worked hard and established himself not only in these streets locally but across state lines. He'd be damned if he allowed Danny to mess it up. However, he needed to keep Danny in his good graces, at least for the time being.

"Yeah, nigga, you heard right. Word on the street is that you jacked one of Barnes' boys. The fuck is you jacking niggas for, bro?"

"Damn! I knew that bitch was gonna recognize my voice. That nigga don't know it was me, does he? You need to teach that hoe to keep her mouth shut, man."

"Keeping her mouth shut ain't what you need to be worried about, bro. She not the one who told me, and you still ain't answered my question. Man, the fuck you doing jackin' niggas? I give enough, so you should have no reason for pulling moves like that."

"You sure doing a lot of talking on this phone. That ain't like you, and that shit is making me paranoid. What's up with that?"

"Paranoid? Ya know what, man? Go ahead and change the subject all you want, but somebody's got the answer for that foul ass shit you did. Unless, of course, you're gonna make things right."

"Make things right, huh? And just how do you suppose I do that?"

"You put some work in, muthafucka. That's how. If you don't want to do that, then I'm gonna have to leave you to face the consequences by your fucking self. I can't keep standing in the mud with you when my boots is the only ones getting dirty. You know what I'm saying?"

The line went silent for a minute, which let Jamir know that Danny was contemplating what he had just said. Jamir already knew what he would decide because, without his backing, Danny was a nobody in the game. Jamir had put him on and tried to keep him on ever since they were jits. He hated the fact that Danny had no respect for him or the streets, but he'd better learn something quickly.

"I know exactly what you're saying, so why don't we meet up and talk about what needs to be done?"

"That's cool, bro. I'll be on the side of Old Man Nat's place waiting for you. And Danny, yo' ass better show up!"

Jamir ended the call and threw his phone onto the seat. When he drove away from Erica's apartment, his sister came to his mind. He still couldn't believe Missy was gone. He had imagined himself one day walking her down the aisle to a man who truly loved and respected her, but that would never be. He regretted not spending more time with her. It was too late to get time back, but it would never be too late to avenge her.

Jamir pulled into Old Man Nat's and parked. No sooner than he shut off his engine, the fiends began showing up, but he didn't have anything for them today, so he shooed them away. The fiends looked disappointed but knew not to stick around and test him either. They had been so used to Jamir parking in that spot when he was making moves, but they also knew that his 'no' was solid, so they cut their losses and walked away in hopes of finding another dealer that would break them off as good as Jamir did.

That night, Jamir had a different agenda and wasn't even thinking about money. Hell, he was up and could stand to lose a few dollars. He could actually take some time off from the streets and still be ok, but the streets were what he loved.

As Jamir sat and waited for Danny to show up, his nose flared. He'd been waiting for almost an hour, and each minute that passed made him even angrier. He had grown sick of running behind Danny and cleaning up his bullshit. It was past time for that nigga to stand up and take some responsibility for his fuck ups. If Danny didn't want to do that, then Jamir had to decide to finally wash his hands of him.

Just as Jamir had given up and was about to start up his car and leave, Danny pulled up beside him. Jamir let out a sigh of frustration and shook his head. As soon as Danny slid into the front seat, he went in.

"The fuck is up with you, nigga? All this disrespectful ass shit you're doing is uncalled for, and I ain't about to keep letting it go. And where the hell have you been at? I've been sitting here, waiting on you for like an hour, man."

"Hold up, bro. Why are you talking to me like I'm one of your foot soldiers? I don't answer to you. Shit, I thought we were equals."

"Equals! Equals? Hell nah! That's what you say, but it ain't what you show. You see, I'm out here pulling money moves, while you pulling jack moves. I'll push keys while you push dick. You acting like an underdog, but me? I'm a top dog, so we far from equals, and as long as you keep tripping like that, the scales gonna stay uneven, my boy."

"Ohh, come on, Jamir. That nigga had it coming. If I wouldn't have pulled that move, someone else would have."

"Then you should have let them. The last thing our team needs is some more enemies. I don't know about you, but where it is, I already got one."

"Well shit, if that's the case, just tell me who it is, and I'll take that muthafucka out for you."

"You sure? Then go ahead and commit suicide, my nigga."

Danny paused for a second to catch on. Jamir could see it. Once Danny let the words that had been spoken marinate in his brain, he became more defensive of Jamir, and that was a sign of guilt, and that was all Jamir needed. He had never been the type of dude to listen to some hood gossip, but because of the look on Danny's face, he knew the rumors were true. However, he knew Danny well enough to know that he was about to feed him a bowl of shit.

"Mir, you funny, dude. You should know by now that I'm the last person you gotta worry about. Now come on and tell me who it was so that I can get at them."

"In so many words, I already did. Word came to me that it was really you on the other end of that call with Raw. I spoke to Malcolm, and that nigga ain't even know. I felt that shit that happened. I've been avoiding his ass for nothing, plotting on that nigga for no reason."

"And you actually believe anything that muthafucka was saying?"

"And I don't have any reason not to. I've been dealing with Malcolm for a while, and he ain't never did me dirty. He ain't got nothing to gain from taking me out. Shit, he would lose out more than he would gain."

"He ain't never did you dirty? Mir, yo' ass tripping for real. If my black ass remembers correctly, that nigga fucked that white bitch you so crazy about. You was supposed to bash his skull in then. If he do some shit like that, he's liable to do anything."

"So, what you're saying is, what I was told wasn't real?"

"You damn right, it was some bullshit. I'm the one that saved your asses that night. Would I have done that if I wanted to take you out or fuck you up in the game? Think about what you're saying. Mir, that don't even sound right. I'm your boy, and I would never betray you like that."

Jamir knew that Danny was lying, deep down, and he wanted him to admit it, but that would take some work. He regretted even bringing it up because, even though Danny denied any involvement, he would now be on alert, and the last thing Jamir needed was a paranoid ass nigga around him, so he decided to diffuse the situation.

"Come on, bro. You know I'm just shooting off at the mouth, talking a little shit, checking to make sure that your loyalty still lies with me."

"What? My loyalty? Don't try me like that, Mir. You and I have been boys a long time, and other than myself, you're the only muthafucka I'm loyal to. I know and understand the code, and I know what you expect from a partner. You ain't gonna never find another muthafucka like me."

"You right, D. The thing is, I don't wanna find another muthafucka like you, because one of you is plenty. It's just crazy how every time something happens with me or someone I care about, your name comes up. Guess that's just a coincidence, though, huh?"

"No. I'm gonna tell you what it is. Muthafuckas is just jealous because I'm your righthand and not them. You know plenty niggas got beef with me because of the way I be dickin' their bitches down. They trying to turn you against me in hopes that they can take my spot. They really believe that shit's gonna happen, but it ain't, and you need to let them know that when they come at you with that drama."

"I don't need to let a nigga know shit. You just need to lay down on that jack shit, sit your ass down, and stop running in on muthafuckas who ain't did a damn thing to you. Know what I'm saying?"

"A'ight, Mir, damn. I hear you, my nigga. And you ain't gonna have to worry about anyone stepping to you again. You have my word on that. So, we're good now?"

"Yeah, D. We good for now. And for your sake, let's hope shit stays that way."

Jamir knew that Danny understood the threat and hoped he didn't take it lightly. Jamir knew there was truth to everything he'd heard, but he needed Danny to admit it, but Danny was a pussy and would never do that. Whatever he had to do to cover up anything he'd done, he'd do.

Jamir waited to start up his ride until Danny got into his and drove off. He hated the fact he had to be cautious of a nigga he'd known for so long. But that was just the way things had turned out.

Jamir couldn't sit there and waste time thinking about it. He was tired and was ready to lie down for the night to get some rest, but he vowed, when he woke up, he would get to the bottom of everything, even if he had to take some lives to do it.

Chapter 14

Danny leaned his head back while he sat on the bed. He looked up at the ceiling and tried to relax his troubled mind while Cassie went to work on his manhood. The bitch could definitely suck the hell out of a dick, but it wasn't enough to keep the thoughts of killing Tomeka out of his mental.

Jamir may not have admitted it, but Danny was certain it was she who fed him the information. The only other person who knew the truth about that night was dead and gone, so Danny knew there was no way he could have snatched him up.

When Danny's thoughts suddenly shifted to Trish and his babies, he became angry and pushed Cassie off his dick. She wiped her mouth and gave him a discerning look. She had grown tired of his in-and-out attitude, but still, she just couldn't leave him alone. She had no freedom when it came to Danny, unlike her man, who wanted to calculate her every move.

"Damn, Danny. Baby, why are you tripping?"

"'Cause all you wanna do is stay on this nigga dick, but I ain't in the mood for that right now. Why don't you go get us something to eat? Or cook a freaking meal? You do you know how to do that, right?"

"Look, I don't know who the hell you think you're talking to like that. I ain't Trish. I'm just trying to comfort you and make you feel good, but I can go and find another man to do that if you won't."

"Well, take your ass on then. I got my boy about to stop by anyway, and I don't need you all up in my business."

"Your boy? Don't let me find out you like dick, because I promise I will shame your black ass to everyone on the block."

"Yeah, you would, with your childish ass. You knew what it was with us when we first hooked up. Don't start getting in your feelings when a nigga don't wanna be bothered. I can get pussy anywhere. I need a bitch that got some sense by my side, and since you don't have any of that, you can bounce."

Cassie didn't move. She just sat there with an attitude. She knew that she had overstepped her boundaries by saying the things she said, but Danny had made her feel like shit. She knew that he was still grieving his losses, but damn. How much longer?

Pouting and lowkey hurt, she stood up. She didn't feel like dealing with his attitude anymore that night anyway. Cassie gathered her clothes and began getting dressed while Danny sat and watched her with a blank stare. She hoped he'd at least try to stop her, but that didn't happen.

"So, it's like that now, Danny? If I leave out this door, there is no coming back. And I mean this, on some real shit."

Danny gave her the coldest stare she'd ever seen from him, and then he smiled. His mood swings were shifting so much lately, and all Cassie could do was shake her head. She never understood men, and she'd be damned if she continued to try to understand them either. She was hurt and began to turn the knob on the door.

She released a long, noticeable sigh, then grabbed her bag, making sure Danny saw all that he would be missing. She bent over and picked up her Jimmie Choo six-inch heels from the floor. She looked over her shoulder one more time to make sure he saw the arch in her back and the jiggle of her round, plump ass. She turned the top lock and began to pull the door open.

"Cassie, baby, you know a nigga just been down for a minute. I don't mean any of this bullshit; on God, I don't. It's just that I'm trying to process a lot. Now, put your shit down and come back in this bed. A nigga got something hard he wanna put in you, baby."

"What about your boy? I thought you said he was about to stop by."

"Now, that is true, but I think I got enough time to wet that pussy up before he get here."

Cassie giggled and dropped her things on the floor. She hoped Danny would come to his senses and ask her to stay because the truth was she didn't want to go home. Her man was out of town again, and she didn't feel like being alone. She quickly undressed and hopped on Danny, full of excitement and love. As they embraced getting to have some make-up sex, there was a knock at the door.

"Aye, why don't you go in the bathroom and freshen up while I take care of some business real quick?"

Feeling a little frustrated, Cassie smacked her lips, but she knew to do as told. She'd been around enough niggas to know her role and stand in her position, meaning business always came first. She had to use the bathroom anyway. "A'ight. I got to piss anyway. But please, Danny, make it quick 'cause I gots to have me some of you."

"I will, and that's my word."

Cassie rushed into the bathroom and shut the door. Danny began to put on his jeans he picked up from the side of the bed. He didn't want to answer the door for his boy naked. He knew, although niggas acted hard as hell on the street, a lot of them indulged in bisexual activity.

"'Sup, nigga? 'Bout time you made it. What took yo' ass so long?

"Shit, you better be glad I even made it at all 'cause I hadn't planned on coming back to town until the weekend. Plus, traffic was crazy out there too, but I gotta admit, the trip was worth it. You will be happy to know that I found out what we needed to know."

"What? Damn right, my nigga. So what's the word? Tell me what I wanna know. Who did that fool-ass shit to my lady and my seeds? Man, I wanna know 'cause that shit should have been the first thing outta yo' mouth."

"A'ight, I'ma tell you, but I need your word that you won't make a move without me. This hit has to be planned step by step. We can't just go in all halfcocked, 'cause if we miss this, we may not get another chance at the muthafucka."

"Yeah, yeah, yeah, you got my word. Now tell me who the fuck it is."

"Well, my people put in word like you asked. Word is that it was the muthafucka that used to roll with Raw. You know that nigga I'm talkin' about?"

"Are you talkin' about that nigga named Blount or some shit like that? I forgot all about that muthafucka."

"That's exactly who I'm talkin' about, and forgetting about that nigga cost my people they lives. Muthafuckas is saying you the one that killed that dyke bitch. That nigga out on some get-back type shit, so he touched you where he knew you was weak, and that was yo' girl and yo' seeds. He went far as fuck, and he gonna have to answer for that."

"Muthfucka! Oh, yeah, he gonna have to see me. I put that on everything. He gonna feel me. My girl and my seeds? Oh, hell nawl! They didn't have shit to do with shit, man. He violated me in the worst way, all over some get-back shit for that dyke bitch? I put that on every fuckin' thing, I'ma see him soon."

"Danny, man, don't you worry. That was my family, and I won't rest until I get that pack back for them. I'll put the word out, and once I get a place and time, then we gon' make that move. For now, though, I got to get up outta here and take my ass home. I been tracking this down too long."

"Aye, bro. Why you don't stick around and chill for a minute? I got a cute hottie in the bathroom freshenin' that thang up. This bitch fine as fuck, and her head game is top tier. I might as well let a nigga reward you for that info."

"Thanks for the offer, but no thanks. I'ma have to pass on that. I got a good woman at home, and she's enough for me. I came back in town early and picked up some flowers and her favorite champagne—a nigga feeling a lil' romantic and shit. I know she be lonely when I be gone like this, so I'ma make it up to her. Ya know what I mean."

"A'ight, but let me be the first to tell you, you missin' out on some grade-A good shit."

"That sound good and all, but ain't nothing out here can top what I got at home, so you gon' 'head and help yo'self. I'm taking my ass to the crib," he said, shaking his head from side to side at Danny's heartless gesture.

He'd been offered plenty of things, but another man's pussy was never one of them. Although the offer would have sounded good to the next man, Denard passed. He never had the desire to be a dog-ass nigga.

The two men shook hands, giving a silent agreement to make this move that would get revenge on Trisha and her kid's murderer. When he began walking out the door, he came in and noticed a pair of custom Jimmie Choo shoes with a matching bag. The one-of-a-kind design was only given to a few people who had this particular set.

His curiosity consumed him as he bent down and picked up one of the heels. Once inspecting it, there was no mistaking it. There was no way he could leave without looking inside of the heel, hoping what he was holding and seeing wasn't true. He was praying that this was a mistake. The initials inside were embroidered. He stood up, holding the heel in his hand to face Danny.

"Ya know what? I changed my mind. Maybe I will stay and have some fun. 'Cause any bitch that owns a pair of these has to be a classy one."

"Oh, she real classy, my nigga, and a true freak, too. Gon' get comfortable while I hurry her ass up."

Danny was so focused on the freakiness that was about to go on that he hadn't noticed Denard's demeanor had shifted. Denard chose to stand where he was as Danny motioned for him to follow him. He examined the heel one more time. He wanted to make sure who he was about to meet would justify his anger. Just when he was about to drop the heel back on the floor, Danny came from the bathroom with a naked female behind him.

"So, this what you do when a nigga out of town, trying to provide you with a good life?"

Denard's tone was angry and hurt, with many more emotions at that moment. He felt every emotion a nigga could feel.

Cassie was afraid, and the look on her face said as much. "Denard, I-I-I... Baby, I'm sorry." Cassie managed to utter her words, and she knew that her worst nightmare was coming to reality at that moment.

Danny looked dumbfounded at what was unfolding in front of him. "Aye, yo, what the fuck goin' on here? Am I missing something?"

"You ain't missin' shit, bruh. It was me that was doin' the missin' out, I see. These Jimmie Choos..." Denard spoke as he pointed toward the heel on the floor, "You see, I had them muthafuckas custom made for this bitch's small ass feet. I even went the extra step and got her initials embroidered inside. I mean, them shits is one of a kind, made just for her funky ass. There wasn't shit I wouldn't do to make this bitch smile. But I see that wasn't enough, since she over here with you."

"Man, listen. I didn't know this was your bitch. I wouldn't have ever crossed that line, bro, for real. If I would have known she was yours, I would have never touched her." Danny looked at Cassie with a frown on his face.

"It's all good, playa. I know her low-down, dusty ass didn't tell you. Just look at her. Ain't she pretty? Any man would have tapped her ass. I mean, that big ass and round hips? Oh, and that star-shaped birthmark on the center of her back is sexy than a muthafucka. Yeah, she that bitch. I ain't gonna hold you accountable, 'cause bitches gon' be bitches, right? But from here on out, this bitch is mine, and you ain't to fuck around with her triflin' ass no more. You cool with that?"

"You fuckin' right, I'm cool with that. As a matter of fact, you can take her with you now."

"Nawl, I'm good on that. Why don't you pass this bitch around like you was about to give to me. I'm done. I got a replacement."

Cassie stood there looking at the both of them as they talked about her like she wasn't shit but gum on the bottom of their shoe. She couldn't believe just how small this world was and the fact she'd been caught up like this. Knowing she had lost all the good life she had in a desperate attempt, she rushed over to Denard as he was turning to walk out the door.

He didn't want her to touch him or even hear her voice. He pushed her down to the floor. She knew he was hurt because he had never put his hands on her out of anger before.

"I'm sorry. Please give me another chance. I know this is no excuse, but you left me alone so much. I just wanted and needed someone to fill the void. I swear I'm so sorry, baby, please. I can't lose you."

Denard gave Cassie a disgusted look. How could he forgive her? As much as he loved her, if she did it once, she would do it again. "Hell nah. Ain't no forgiving this shit right here. No, baby girl. Take yo' ass on with that shit, for real. Was you thinking of losing me when you was fuckin' this nigga? Hell no, you wasn't. 'Cause if you was, yo' stupid ass would have never done it. You played yo'self. Now, all yo' shit gonna be on the front porch, and just know you leaving with only the shit you came with."

Cassie collected her belongings and walked toward the door, hoping someone would ask her to stay. Both Danny and Denard stood there, looking as she glanced in their direction one more time before leaving them behind.

Chapter 15

Jamir sat in the cut, bobbing his head to the music. The bass from 'Ready for War' by ASAP Preach, Nicky Gracious, and Rave of Breed was strong. He had never gravitated to the new wave of Christian rap, but he had to give it to those crackers; they damn sure hit some bars on this cut. Each lyric seemed to hit his soul. He felt like he could relate in so many ways. Jamir knew there were muthafuckas that wanted him out of the way. That gave him no other choice but to stay ready so he wouldn't have to get ready. He never knew the time or day one of them snakes would come for him and all he had built, so he had to stay on point.

The block had been quiet for most of the night. There had only been one good rush of things, but once they were served, shit seemed to die down. Jamir looked at the time and saw it was still too early to take it in. He wasn't in a rush to go home anyway, because there would be nothing waiting for him there. His grandmother and Missy were both gone, Rachel was still locked up, and Danny was on that bullshit. All Jamir had was himself, and at times, he wondered if that was enough.

The bright lights caught Jamir by surprise. Police presence had never really been heavy in that area because they didn't give a damn. However, Jamir didn't feel like having a run-in with one of them.

He took a deep breath and prepared himself for whatever was about to unfold. He had dope and money on him, but he also had a pistol. He could handle a possession charge because he didn't have a serious enough amount to send him away for long, but that gun charge could do some real damage.

Jamir let out a sigh of relief. He didn't know who was driving the vehicle, but he'd rather deal with a stranger than the boys in blue. Jamir put his hand on his nine and gripped the handle just in case he needed to pull it out, but once he realized who it was, he eased his hold.

Jamir hit the button to unlock his door as soon as Blount tapped on the window. The breeze from the night filled the inside of Jamir's ride. As soon as Blount opened the door and jumped in, Jamir already knew what he was there for: some answers. Blount lost someone dear to him, so Jamir completely understood that.

"'Sup, Jamir? I ain't up here with no type of beef and shit, my nigga. I just need to know what happened to my people, man."

"No, you're good, bro, but your people turned foul on me."

"I heard all that, but from what I understand, your boy turned foul as fuck, too. The part I don't get is why the fuck he played Raw and then took her out for some shit he had set up himself. Can't say it was to protect you, because we both know that muthafucka wants to be where you at. He just knows he ain't gonna ever make it there as long as you're in the game."

Jamir could only nod his head because he knew the words Blount spoke were nothing but the truth. He'd always known of Danny's jealousy of him. He just couldn't understand the reason behind it. Jamir had always been fair to that nigga, but he guessed it just wasn't enough and probably never would be.

"Alright, let me be straight up with you. I used to sit back and watch Raw work. To me, that nigga looked to be as real as they come. That was the main reason I stepped to her in the first place. I wanted to form a tight circle in my crew, and I felt like she was the missing link. You can't even imagine how I felt when she turned snake on me. Yeah, she was cutting paper before me, but you know for yourself that I laced those pockets up right. I'm a fair ass nigga, always have been, and always will be. I don't mind putting food on the table, and I always put enough on everyone's plate. A nigga would never go hungry, fuckin' with me. That's why I don't get why your girl went out on me like that."

"Look. I can't explain to you why she did what she did, but she didn't do that shit alone. I been here, and I would have never let her make a move like that. But your boy had to kill her, though."

"The fuck you mean? It was her or me. I showed that muthafucka love, and that shit wasn't appreciated or reciprocated in the end. She returned that shit with envy and hate. I had major plans for the whole crew, and no one was gonna be left behind. We was about to take this street shit over. All I ever wanted to see us all rise above our ghetto ass circumstances. I'm a muthafuckin' team player. I just can't understand why everyone else can't or won't be. It's enough money out here for us all."

"I don't understand. I feel where you're coming from, bro. I really do. But you ain't gonna never have a strong team as long as your boy is in his position. That nigga don't mean you no good, and as soon as I get a clear shot, I'm gonna take his ass out. I only came here to let you know about it so you stay out of the way. If you choose to get involved, that's on you. Just know the consequences behind it."

Jamir was less impressed that Blount came to him this way and pretty much issued a threat if he chose to help Danny. He almost let his nine sing before Blount got out of his ride. Instead, Blount opened the door and got out. He didn't wait for a response because what he said didn't warrant one. In his mind, it was what it was, and nothing and nobody was gonna change it. He was going to kill Danny one way or another. The last thing Blount wanted was to start a street war, but if that's what it came to, he would.

Jamir laughed to himself as he watched Blount run to his ride, jump in, and speed off. He truly began to believe that the niggas around the block thought he was a pussy. Jamir walked away from so many muthafuckas that had brought bullshit to his feet because he never wanted to be a killer. Right then and there, he decided the days of muthafuckas testing him were over. The next one that stepped to him on some King-Kong type shit was gonna pay. He didn't care if it was a small threat. They were gonna feel it.

Jamir noticed a light tap on his window, pulling him from his thoughts. He couldn't believe he let someone else get close enough to him to tap on his window. He had been so in his thoughts he didn't notice until it was too late.

His intense emotions eased a little as he looked at the pretty female at his window. He could have sworn he'd seen her somewhere before. He wasn't sure where, but to be on the safe side, he placed his hand on his nine-millimeter he held in his waistband. If she came at him wrong, she would be the first one to get it. As soon as she noticed his weapon, she held her arms up, just letting him know she wasn't there for any trouble. Jamir slowly put his window down while he continued to hold on to his gun.

"What's up? You need something?"

"Please, if you can just give me a ride to my friend Syleena's house, I would be very grateful. I feel like I've been walking all night, and my feet are killing me."

Jamir noticed the expensive Jimmy Choo heels in her hand and became even more skeptical. The bitch had a good-paying job, or she had a nigga that didn't mind spending that gwap. He was almost certain that it was the latter. He figured that she and her man had some issues, and instead of working them out, she dipped on him. The last thing Jamir wanted was to get caught up in a love triangle, but he couldn't just leave her hanging.

"The fuck is you doing out here this time of night? Where yo' man that anyway? And don't tell me your pretty ass ain't got one."

"I had one up until about two hours ago, when he decided to bring his black ass back to town early and caught me with the next man. I thought he was gonna be my new man, but boy was a bitch."

"Whoa, no wonder yo' ass out here walkin'. You lucky he didn't beat yo' ass. I'm guessing yo' man wasn't doin' his part. 'Cause if he was, you wouldn't have auditioned a new nigga."

Smacking her lips, she said, "Look. I need a ride to my girl's crib. That's all. I didn't stop and ask you for a one-on-one counseling session. You all up in my business. Are you gonna help me out or nawl?"

"Look, you came to me, and because I ain't one of these niggas that wanna see a pretty bitch like yourself strugglin', come on. Get yo' whining ass in the car. I'ma let you know right now, if you pull some bullshit, I'ma push yo' wig back. You understand?"

"Thank you, and yeah, I understand. But just so you know, everything on me is real, including this hair. This shit is all mine."

The female rolled her eyes, walked over to the passenger side of Jamir's car, and got in. She looked defeated and angry, wondering just how she allowed herself to be played like a simple bitch by a nigga. She just felt the best thing for her to do at the moment was stay quiet and get the ride she needed. She didn't want to give him any more reasons to ask questions she wasn't prepared to answer. She didn't have the energy for an interrogation. She felt she did nothing wrong. She was grown and would take her fuck-up like a real G, but she didn't wanna talk about it.

"Ya know? You look real familiar to me. Do I know you from somewhere? At least tell me who you are, 'cause I don't normally give strangers a ride."

Looking a little complexed, she said, "No, I don't think so, and that just might be a good thing. If you don't mind, can you be done with the questions? I'm sorry. I really don't have the energy to relive what happened tonight."

"Hell nawl. That ain't how that shit gon' work. You up in my shit, and I ain't done with the questions. A nigga like me need to know who the hell up in my shit. I just ain't no Captain Save-A-Hoe. You obliviously ain't shit, since you jumped to the next man. Yo' man leave out of town, making shit happen for y'all to eat, and judging by those pricey heels in your hands, you live a good life, no doubt. You females can't be loyal for shit, always wanting more when y'all have everything."

"You know what? Fuck you! Fuck you! Fuck you! Let me out. I'll just walk. At least you can save some gas money."

Jamir felt her emotions and sat there, waiting to see if she was really going to get out of the car. She continued to sit there and sulk. He could tell the situation really messed her up mentally. Jamir decided to cut her slack and take her where she needed to go. Although he didn't know her, he really didn't want her to have to walk, because it might risk her getting into someone else's ride, possibly getting her raped or hurt. Jamir wouldn't be able to live with himself if something happened to her.

"Alright, I'm gonna chill with all the questions, but don't you think that I have a right to know who I got up in my shit? I mean, I got muthafuckas trying to take me out of the game. They seem to want my spot, and they got a nigga paranoid, and I can't afford to lose focus. You know what I'm saying?"

"Ok, well damn. Since you put it that way, my name is Cassie, and I apologize for being such a bitch to you, but I'm the one who needs the favor. I'm really not a bad person just because I did what I did. It's just that my man never stayed at home. And a girl gets lonely. I needed someone. And I know they're my friends and all, but I didn't want to hang around Syleena and Chanel all the time. The only thing they bring to the table is gossip and drama. I don't have time for that. I got lonely, and I needed somebody who could put me first. That's all. And no, that's no excuse, but if that makes me a hoe or whatever, oh well. So be it. I just feel like I deserved that much."

"It takes a real person to admit when they're wrong, and I can't do nothing but respect that. Well, let me ask you a question if that's ok. Who is your man, or what's your man's name?"

"Yeah, it's cool. That nigga's name is Denard Gaston, but you probably don't know him because he does all his business out of town. Don't ask me what kind of business it is, because honestly, I do not know. It could be drugs or anything. I don't know. I don't question him, though, because I'd rather not know that shit. The last thing I want is for someone to use me against him. You know they always say when somebody strong, especially in the game, they always got a weakness, and they always seem to go after a nigga's bitch."

"Ok, ok, smart girl. I see Denard groomed you very well. By the way, I do know him. I mean not personally, but I've known of him for a long time. I just never really opted to fuck with him like that on business. Now I'm glad that I never tried."

"And why is that? He ain't no bad person or anything. That shit was my fuck-up, not his."

"Nah, that ain't even what I'm saying. I just don't want a muthafucka to feel some type of way because his bitch is in my front seat."

"Would you rather for me to sit in the back seat?" Jamir smiled at Cassie. There was just something about the way she said it that made his dick get hard. He hadn't been in some pussy for a minute, but it would be another minute before he did.

Cassie had acquired enough problems on her own without him getting in the mix. He wasn't about to get caught up in the middle of that. Plus, if the things he heard about Denard were true, he would rather make him an ally than an enemy.

"I'm not quite sure what you meant by that comment, but we gonna act like you never said it."

Cassie rolled her eyes and giggled but didn't respond. She was tired and couldn't wait to be dropped off. Once Jamir pulled into the apartment complex she had given him directions to, she quickly gathered her things. She was in a hurry to get away from this nigga that had her pussy soaking wet. Cassie knew she was wrong, but his bossed-up attitude turned on. She had been on the verge of offering him some, but she wanted to leave him with some kind of respect for her.

When Jamir's ride finally came to a stop, Cassie opened the door to get out, but she paused because she knew that she had to at least thank him for his time. She never knew if she would run into him again, so she wanted to part on good terms.

"Thank you for everything. I really appreciate it. I know you didn't have to do it, and I want you to know that if you ever see me around again, and I can help you with anything, please don't hesitate to ask. I'm not a bad person. I just made bad choices."

Jamir nodded his head, but before he let her step completely out of the vehicle, he had one more question for her. "Hey, wait. I do have one more thing I'd like to ask you if that's ok."

"Sure, go ahead. That's the least I can do. Plus, I've already told you so much."

"I just wanna know, who was the other nigga you were sliding on your man with?"

Cassie pressed her lips together, but then she answered him. "His name was Danny Jacobs. I should have never messed around with him. But that's the nigga's name."

Chapter 16

Denard sat alone in the VIP booth and nursed a fat blunt that he rolled only minutes before. He never really cared to smoke in public places, but since he no longer had a reason to go home, he opted to chill at the strip club. It had been a place he'd avoided for a very long time, but since Cassie was no longer a part of his life, he didn't owe her that anymore. Denard felt like he could live a little and do whatever he wanted since he didn't have to answer to anyone anymore.

It felt kind of nice to be on his own, but he couldn't lie to himself. He missed the hell out of Cassie. He thought she would be the one he would give his last name to. Denard, who had invested so much of his time and money on her, but now, he had to count his losses and walk away. Out of all the niggas she could have slid on him with, she had to choose Danny. She didn't know Danny was his cousin's man, but even still, there was no way he could look past that indiscretion.

Just as Denard blew out a mouthful of smoke, something caught his eye. He wasn't sure how to react to the situation that had unfolded right in front of him. He had been good to Cassie, so nothing made any sense. True enough, she was her own woman. Due to the dumb choices she had made, watching her grind on the next man's lap bothered him.

The longer Cassie swayed her hips back and forth, the more irate Denard became. She did it like a pro and had done it before. He was so angry that he was ready to bust a cap in that bitch's head for the open disrespect, but he decided that she really wasn't even worth the bullet.

Denard took another pool of the Purple Rain Kush before he and Cassie locked eyes. They stared at each other for what seemed like forever. His stare was full of anger and hurt, while hers was full of regret. As bad as Denard wanted to get up and leave, something inside of him made him stay. He knew he made Cassie uncomfortable, but her comfort was no longer his concern. Denard finally broke the stare and turned his focus elsewhere. He saw the snow bunny coming his way, and when she stopped in front of him, he smiled. He knew that nothing would piss Cassie off more than for him to accept time from a white girl. He'd never lain down with one, but he heard they were really freaky. But if things worked out the way he hoped, he was about to find out.

"'Sup, Snow? You feel like getting your grind on? A nigga got some of that purp and plenty of money to spend. That is if you up to it."

"Umm, sounds like I came to the right table. I'm gonna put on a nice show just for you. And who knows? Maybe when I'm done, you'll join me in the back for a real deal."

"Shit, my dick pulsating already. Go ahead and bust that move, lil' mama."

The white girl smiled and popped the latch on her top so that her breasts could breathe. Denard could tell off the rip that they were fake because of how perfectly they sat up. He didn't mind it, though, because to him, titties were just titties, and as soon as she mounted herself backward on him, he reached around and pinched her handful of her nipples. They felt fat and juicy between his fingers, and as good as he wanted to suck on one of them, he decided to pass.

Denard glanced over at Cassie. He could feel her eyes boring into him as the white girl danced and worked her magic on his lap. Her ass bounced to the beat of the music while he licked his lips and thought about how he was going to nut all over her pale skin. Denard tried but couldn't resist reaching his hand between her legs. Her pussy was fat. As he ran a finger along the fabric of her thong, he could feel the wetness that had already begun. Denard pulled his hand back and patted her on the ass he was ready to do some damage.

"Damn, Snow. You got a nigga on swole. What's up with that backroom action?"

"I thought you'd never ask. Come on and follow me, Big Daddy."

The dancer stood and grabbed Denard's hand, but before he had a chance to stand, another voice stopped him.

"You can let his hand go now, bitch, because he ain't going nowhere with you."

The white girl gave Cassie a dirty look and then looked at Denard to say something. No defense, but when he let her hand go, she knew what was up. It wasn't the first customer Cassie had stolen from her, and it probably wouldn't be the last, but since she didn't have time to play those types of games, she just walked away. She was sure there were other big ballers in the building, and she wouldn't stop until she found her one.

Denard looked at Cassie like she'd lost her mind. She had some nerve to think that she could regulate anything when it came to him. The female he thought was a lady turned out to be nothing but a hoe, and he would treat her as such. He owed her no more respect, and she would soon find that out.

"Bitch, who the fuck is you to walk over here and control a damn thing? You lost that privilege when you let another nigga run up in my pussy."

"Wow, Denard. You have never talked to me like this before. Do you really think I deserve it? I'm sorry for hurting you, but please let me make it up to you."

"You wanna make it up? Get naked, and slide on this dick—right here, right now. Shouldn't be too hard for you to do that since somehow, that's suddenly your profession."

"No, I didn't wanna fuck that man that came up in here. Things just happened. When Danny showed up one night, it just got out of hand. I know that ain't no excuse, but hell, I don't have one. I'm woman enough to own up to my part."

Denard thought about what Cassie said. He thought he had misunderstood, but from the sound of it, she had met Danny at this very club.

"The fuck you mean, when Danny showed up? How long you been doing this shit?"

Cassie lowered her head. "For about seven months, but I would only work on the nights I knew you'd be out of town."

"Seven months? Seven fuckin' months, you've been out here shaking your ass for other muthafuckas? All that time, and I didn't know about it. The hell was you doing it for? Couldn't have been for the money because, bitch, I kept your purse loaded."

"Look, Denard. I'm gonna keep it real. It's not always about the money. I told you that I was lonely. I came and danced here because I liked the attention that the other men gave me—the attention I couldn't get from you."

"The hell out of here with all that bullshit. You know how many bitches would love to have been in your shoes?"

"I do, Denard. I do know. I never deserved a man like you, yet you gave me a chance, and I failed you. I was weak to Danny's advances, and I know that. I can't take it back, but let me make it up to you. We can make it like it was once again."

"Make it like it was? You serious? But you did know that my cousin was Danny's baby mama, right? I don't fuck behind niggas I know. And was you aware that the night I came to that room, his ass offered you up to me, not knowing that you already belonged to me? Huh? How does it make you feel to know that you was muthafuckin' nothing? He was ready to pass you off to me to run a train on your trifling ass. Danny couldn't care less about you. That nigga get plenty of pussy. Did you think he would settle with just you? Come on, baby girl. You can't be that dumb."

"You ain't never talked to me like this before. I mean, I know I was wrong, but I don't deserve to be done like this. Yeah, I fucked up. People make mistakes, but had your ass been at home like you should have been, nothin' might've ever happened."

"You're right. You deserve far worse than this. Wasn't shit I wouldn't have done for you. And if only you would have told me you wanted more of my time, you would have got it. You were my world, Cassie, and everything I did, I did it for you."

He towered over the woman he thought he'd marry one day. She stared up at him with a look of desperation, and it made his heart beat twice. Denard finally bent down and kissed her on the forehead, a sweet, romantic gesture he always did before he left home to go anywhere. As soon as he did it, Cassie reached out for him.

Denard lightly pushed her away and then reached into his pocket. He pulled out a small black box and held it out in front of her. He had bought the ring on his way back to town. He planned to give it to her and ask her to be his wife. Then he was also going to tell Cassie that it would be his last time leaving her. However, everything had changed.

"I bought this for you because I honestly thought that you'd be mine forever. Shit's crazy how things change so quickly. What once was will never be again. I wanted you to have this anyway. I don't need it anymore. Goodbye, Cassie."

Denard placed the ring box in her hand and walked away. He swore and never looked back. The woman who was his everything was now nothing to him. Denard would move on, and he was sure that Cassie would, too. He walked out of the strip club and inhaled the night air. It was time to hook up with Danny and blow some shit up. When it was all over, only one of them would be left. Denard just hoped it would be him who was still standing.

Chapter 17

Danny had been out on the block serving fiends when Jamir walked up to him aggressively, and it threw him completely off because he had no warning.

"So when did you start fuckin' with bitches that belong to niggas in your circle? I mean, I know you and Denard don't consider yourselves best friends or anything like that, but damn, D. That's your baby momma's cousin. You and I both know that was some shady ass shit, bro. That completely violates the code, man."

"Aye, Mir, fuck a damn code. The hell is wrong with you? I bet you can't stand here and name me one muthafucka that follows that shit. I'm sure your ass done slipped a time or two. Besides, it ain't my fault that Cassie didn't bother to mention who her man was. I found that bitch in the strip club. She was shaking that ass on me, so she was fair game.

"And what if she would have told you that she was Denard's bitch? Huh, D? Would it have made a difference?"

"Shit, I ain't even gonna lie. That hoe pretty as fuck, and she thick with it. Denard had him a prime piece, and any real nigga knows that you can't leave a bitch like that out of your sight for too long. Cassie got lonely, and only a dumb muthafucka would have turned that down. She is a fuckin' masterpiece, and you know it just as well as I do."

"Ohh yeah? Well, I ain't had a problem letting her slip by me. Once she told me who her man was, any and every thought about her went out the window. Shit, just the sight of that bitch made my shit hard as a brick. But no matter what you seem to think, I follow the code."

"She didn't bother to tell me all that, so I'm an innocent participant in all of this. Did she really try you, though? Or you just saying that so that I don't fuck with her no more?"

"You should know me well enough to know that I don't play no games. She told me all about you having her in that room when Denard showed up and recognized some damn shoes that belonged to her. When she left there, she walked up on me over by Nat's. Ohh, my bad. You ain't know that I knew about what happened, but Cassie ass told me everything that went down. She asked me for a ride to her home girl's crib, even offered to get in the back seat, if you know what I mean."

Danny knew that Jamir was telling the truth because there was no way he would have known what happened in that room unless someone who was there told him about it. Danny was pissed, and as soon as he ran into Cassie again, he was going to let her know about it.

"Ohh, so she offered to get in your backseat, huh? And you think that meant something? It really don't. It really don't matter, though, because she don't even know we're affiliated. I'm sure if she knew, she would have never had tried that shit."

"Yeah, that's coming from a nigga that she was cheating on her nigga with. But, yo, that ain't my drama, D. You're the one that gets to face that shit. I got more important things to think about than your dick and its misadventures. I'll get back with you later. I'm out of here."

Jamir turned and walked away without another word, leaving Danny to his thoughts. Danny shook his head and couldn't help but wonder if Jamir was about to go meet up with Malcolm. The thought of it made him angry all over again because he had tried so hard to turn Jamir against Malcolm. Deep down in his gut, he felt like Jamir trusted Malcolm more than him.

Danny really didn't care, though, because if things went the way he hoped, then muthafuckas would be answering to him soon. His time to run things was overdue. He had waited long enough, and if Jamir didn't step down, Danny planned to knock him down. He was tired of being second to anyone else.

Thoughts of Tomeka came to his mind. He had been meaning to visit her and figured it was the perfect time. Danny had some questions for her that he needed answers. He knew she was the one who filled Jamir's ears with what had really happened between him and Raw. Then he cut the lights on in his ride before he pulled into the parking spot in front of Tomeka's building.

Just to be safe, he looked up toward her apartment and noticed that the light was still on. He wondered if she had company or if she was chilling. Danny knew the only way to find out was to get out and knock on her door. He would have called, but he didn't want to spook her or give her a chance to get away. Tomeka had to have known that he would come for her one day. Raw made it seem like the bitch was a loyal rider, but that was not true. Had Danny known sooner, Tomeka would have been dead and would have never had the chance to tell Jamir anything.

No sooner had Danny stepped out of his ride, a fiend named Jimmy came out of the darkness and walked up to him. Danny wasn't alarmed, though, because Jimmy was no stranger to him or to anybody else in that hood. In the hood, at one time in his life, Jimmy had been the man to see, especially if they wanted a good deal. Fiends and dealers, alike, respected him. Jimmy once owned a big home on six acres of land, three luxury vehicles, and he had plenty of pussy on standby. There wasn't a bitch in the state that didn't want to have his baby. In addition, some of Jimmy's diamonds cost more than a Bentley, and muthafuckas looked up to him like he was a real king.

For years, Jimmy ruled the streets. He had all the dope spots on lock, and nobody was mad about it. Jimmy treated everyone the same and blessed those who couldn't help themselves. One day, he met a female named Linda, and his status slowly dissipated. Linda was a bad bitch, and no other female could stand in her shoes. She had a fat ass, slim waist, perky breasts, and long, natural hair. Her green eyes made her peanut-butter-colored skin glow in the dimness, and the fruity perfume she always wore would make niggas' dicks stand at attention.

She was a drug dealer's dream piece, but she was also an addict. One never would have guessed it by her appearance, but Linda hit the pipe as often as she could. At first, she didn't tell Jimmy about it, but as soon as she had him pussy whipped, she revealed what she had kept in the dark. Jimmy was so far gone over her that he didn't even care and began to support her habit, and eventually, she convinced him to try it too. Once Linda had him strung out on his own product, she left him for the next up-and-comer.

However, she made sure his bank account and other assets had been depleted before she left. Jimmy was left not only heartbroken, but broke and addicted too. He went from a major baller to a crackhead, looking for a hit, seemingly overnight.

"Danny, that's you? Damn, nigga. It feels like I ain't seen you in a minute. You looking all clean and shit. I hear you've been doing good for yourself out here, young blood. So why don't you go ahead and help a brother out? I need a little something to top my night off, old friend."

Danny could not believe the sight of him. Jimmy looked like a totally different person. His clothes were dirty and tattered, and his dreads, which used to be clean and neat, were knotted up with a foul odor coming from them. Jimmy's mouth, which was once full of gold, was no longer shiny but had turned brown and smelled like he had just finished eating a corpse. Danny could only back up and shake his head at the sight of him.

"Dayum, Jimmy. Boy, I almost didn't recognize you out here looking like a muthafuckin' scarecrow and shit. And when was the last time you brushed your teeth, nigga? Your breath is on fire."

"Ohh naw. Come on, Danny. I ain't that bad off, family. Just think about what I used to be. You don't need to worry about all that, though, because I'm working on getting back right. Just give me a minute. Watch how I come back up. They're just gonna be hating for real when I step back out on the scene shit, even you."

"I don't know what about all that, but you gonna have to show me. I hope you serious about it, though, because you used to be a deep-on-your-grind type of nigga. I can't believe you let that hoe hook you real bad."

"Yeah, yeah, fuck that bitch. She on to another nigga's nut sack anyway now. I can't wait to see that karma slap her on her ass. Anyway, I just need me a little hit to keep me on my toes, you know? You're gonna look out for me or what?"

Danny shook his head again in disbelief and then reached into his pocket. He thought about himself and how he could have easily ended up just like Jimmy. Danny had dabbled a little in crack high, but after Missy died, he decided to back away from it. Thankfully, he had managed to stay off the pipe without any cravings. Too bad Jamir hadn't been as lucky.

"I'll tell you what. I'm gonna give you this little bit that I got left 'cause when I leave from here, I don't plan on going back out there. But you gotta do me a solid too."

"Ok, Danny, what you need? You wanna get your dick sucked or something? I mean, I ain't the best at it, but the more I practice, the better I get."

"Hell no! It ain't on no homo type of shit. And don't you ever try me like that again, nigga. If you do, I'ma put a hot one in your ass, and I ain't talking about no dick. You feel me?"

"My bad, my bad. I mean, I just do what I gotta do to get what I need. You know what I mean? But on the real, what you need from me, though?"

"I need you to keep your fucking mouth shut if anybody ever asks you was I over here. I got me another nigga's bitch upstairs, and I don't need him finding out I'm bonkin' his hoe. Can you do that?"

"Yeah. Uh, yeah, I know to keep my mouth shut. Don't worry. You can count on me. Go on and bust that nut, and I'm-I'm gonna go bust mine right on this pipe."

Jimmy held up his glass pipe and licked his crusty, chapped lips before he walked back into the same darkness he'd come out of. Danny stood by his ride for a second, patiently waiting for Jimmy to get out of sight before he trotted up the stairs to Tomeka's apartment. When Danny made it to her door, he took another minute to look around. He wanted to make sure that no one else had seen him. When he finally felt like it was safe enough, he knocked on the door and stepped back.

Tomeka had just given herself an ultimate orgasm when she heard the knock at her front door. It seemed that since Raw was gone, no one thought much of her anymore, so she wondered who it could be. She sent a silent prayer up and hoped it would be answered. The last thing she needed was for Blount to show up again.

She had already given him the answers he needed, so he had no reason to bother her again. Plus, her ankles had slowly begun to heal, and she couldn't handle them being broken again. Tomeka was grateful, though, because she had graduated from a wheelchair to crutches. Soon, she would be back on her feet, and she couldn't wait to hit the club.

Tomeka threw her casted foot off the side of the bed just as the knock came again. Whoever it was seemed anxious to see her. She just hoped that she was equally as anxious to see them. She finally put the crutches under her arms and hobbled to the front door. She made sure to step midway through just to take a look in the mirror. She thought to herself it could be some dick, so she wanted to look her best just in case. When Tomeka looked through the peephole and saw who it was, she became disappointed. Her wish for some dick had come true, but it was one that could only last two minutes. However, she still opened the door.

"Hope you brought your Viagra this time because, nigga, I need some dick, and I ain't talking about a quickie."

He was thrown off by what Tomeka said but decided that he might as well hit that pussy before he took her life. He would act like he didn't go there with any beef until he got a good enough nut. After that, he planned to spaz on that bitch.

"Meka, I don't, but I got my little issue taken care of. Now I can hang on a little while longer."

"Ok, come on, Danny. I need my back blew out. I'm tired of playing with myself."

Danny's eyebrows scrunched together, and he then looked at Tomeka up and down. He wondered why he didn't notice the crutches when she first opened the door. He hadn't heard anything about her being in any accident, so the cast she was bound in was a complete mystery to him. That wasn't his problem, though, as long as the pussy still worked.

"Shit, I just had a little fall. That's it, nothing for you to worry about. Just come on in and handle your business."

"Looks like to me you already had a blowout. The hell is up with those crutches and these muthafuckin' casts?"

Danny finally stepped into the apartment but at a slow pace. Something seemed off to him, but he couldn't quite place it. As soon as Tomeka shut her door, he reached for his Glock. After what she had told Jamir, Danny couldn't be too careful.

"Is somebody up in this bitch with you?"

"Danny, come on now. I could assure you that if I had someone up here, I wouldn't have to play in my own pussy.

They would have been doing the job. Besides, why are you so damn paranoid?"

"I ain't paranoid. I just don't know who I can trust anymore. I laugh at this plea of loyalty, knowing all they can really give is solidity. You know what I mean?"

"What the hell is solidity?"

"It's where you done made the word loyalty go sour. You wouldn't happen to know anything about that, though, would you?"

Meka sat in her favorite chair, put her crutches to the side, and then looked up at Danny, who was standing directly in front of her. She was a little taken aback by his question, so instead of answering it, she reached out and unzipped his jeans. When she reached in and pulled out his semi-hard manhood, he just smiled. She knew niggas would forget everything else when it came to getting a nut.

"The only thing I know about right now is showing some loyalty to this dick. Umm, I can't wait to have it inside of me."

"Well, go ahead and get to work 'cause when you're done, I'm gonna hit that spot on that pussy real good, and then daddy gonna give you a nice surprise."

"I can't wait."

"Yeah, I bet yo' ass can't."

Chapter 18

Denard walked out of the strip club with a whole hell of a lot on his mind. The thought of no longer having Cassie in his life had not fully set in yet, but he could tell from the hurt he felt deep in his soul that the shift was real. He just knew, one day, he would stand at the front of their church and smile as he walked her down the aisle. However, after what she'd done with Danny, Denard's future had become his past. He had never been a weak man, but he truly loved the hell out of Cassie, and what she had done would forever haunt his heart. Bitches should beware because Denard no longer gave a fuck.

Just as he was about to open the door to his Navigator, another vehicle pulled up next to him. Any other time, Denard would have reached for his nine, but when he saw that it was Jamir, he knew there would be no need for it. He and Jamir had always been cool, even when he and Danny weren't.

Jamir had never been known as a shady type of dude, and he carried mad respect for him in the hood. Denard wondered why he was at the strip club because that had never really been his thing. Denard waited patiently for Jamir to get out of his ride so he could see what the biz was, not knowing that they had the same thing in mind.

"'Sup, Denard? Funny seeing you here, my man. You ain't happen to see Danny around here anywhere, did you?"

"Well, I would tell you that he was somewhere with my bitch, but since I just seen her up in the club, shaking her ass, I know that would be bad information. I'm actually looking for him myself. He was supposed to meet up with me and handle something, but he ain't answering his phone. Might be out there fuckin' on somebody else's bitch by now."

"Yeah, I heard about what had happened between y'all. Sorry about that, bro. But with a disloyal ass nigga, you don't never know what to expect. Shit, for all I know, he could be my daughter's father."

"Now wouldn't that be some shit?"

"Damn right it would be. But listen, Denard. Since we are here shooting the shit, let me run something by you real quick."

"Alright, I'm listening. What's going on?"

"I know you ain't never really wanted to be put on the grind, but I think you need to do something to get your mind off what happened. I know that shit had to be hard to swallow, and I can see you still choking from it. I could use someone like you on my team, though—someone that I know I can depend on. To keep things real, what do you think about that?"

"That all sounds real good, but you know I ain't never been the type to be out there like that. I'm good on keeping a low profile. That dope-slinging game just ain't for me. Besides, I already got my own thing going on elsewhere, you know what I mean?"

"I got you, and I can only respect that, but what you gonna do? With that Cassie situation?"

"Ain't gonna do a damn thing about it but keep on moving with my life. The saying is true: you can't turn a hoe into a housewife. I just feel bad for any bitch that comes behind her. That's who gonna pay for her bullshit."

"Uh, come on now, bro. You can't hold it against anybody else but her. That shit ain't right. You and I both know that. Besides, you ain't never been the one to dog a hoe, and I can't see you turning into that. You are a good ass nigga, Denard. Just hold on to the hope that the right one will come along. I give you my word on that."

"I hear you talking, but I'm just wondering, is Erica your right one?"

"Hell no. I just ended up being an accidental sperm donor to that hoe. The only good thing that came from that was my little girl. Other than her, we don't share a damn thing. My heart is sitting in the pen as we speak."

"Well, who the hell are you talking about?"

"Well, you gonna find this shit real crazy, but I'm banking on Rachel to have a future with."

"You mean white girl Rachel? Crackhead Rachel?"

"You ain't gotta say it all like that, and nobody is muthafuckin' perfect. She got a few flaws, but ain't nothing that can't be fixed."

"I feel you on that, Jamir. Whatever makes you happy. Now let's see can we find that muthafucka. He can't be too far."

Jamir thought for just a second then had an idea. If Jamir knew Danny the way he knew he knew Danny, then the only time he wouldn't answer the phone is when he was deep in some pussy. Jamir knew exactly where he might be.

"Come on, Denard. I think I know where to find him."

Chapter 19

Tomeka felt Danny's legs begin to shake in front of her. She sucked his dick so good it caused him to tremble. She wasn't a dumb bitch. She knew exactly why he'd shown up to her door. It definitely wasn't for her sex. However, she would suck and fuck him dry if that would buy her some more time.

"Damn, girl. You ain't playin' wit' this muthafucka. I ain't never had a bitch suck my dick this good."

"Yeah, well, what happened? Because you still only lasted a couple of minutes. I don't even know how you can manage to enjoy something that quick. I could have sworn you said that you had that little issue taken care of. Now you ain't even gonna be able to give me what I want. That's real fucked up, Danny."

"You shouldn't have been so damn good at it, and I could have lasted longer. Just give me a minute, and I'll be back right."

"Whatever you say, but while you're taking care of your problem, I gotta go piss. It would be nice if you have that thing working again by the time I get back. I mean, I really do need some dick."

Danny moved out of the way so Tomeka could get around him. She gave him one last look as she picked up her crutches and limped away. She couldn't lie to herself. She did want to get fucked, but a quickie wasn't going to bring her any pleasure at all. That in-and-out shit just wasn't for her.

True enough, she didn't mind laying on her back, but a nigga better come with it or get lost.

Tomeka hobbled into the bathroom and shut the door behind her. She went ahead and locked it too, just in case Danny decided to barge in and check on her. She sat down on the toilet and pulled the shower curtain back.

She knew the shower foam would come in handy one day. She purchased it so she could lay back in the bubble bath and call sex lines. No one knew of her dirty little secret, and she would make sure to keep it that way.

Tomeka quickly dialed the number she had memorized and waited. The phone continuously rang without anyone answering it, and right when she was about to give in and hang up, someone picked up on the other end.

"This better be real damn good."

Tomeka shook her head and then whispered into the phone, "He's here. I think he knows I put the truth out, and he may be trying to kill me. Please get here as fast as you can. I'll hold him off as long as I can."

"Ok, bet. I'm on the way, but it's going to take me a little minute to get there because I'm not close. Do whatever you gotta do to hold the nigga there. You will be rewarded greatly for it."

Before Tomeka could respond, the call was disconnected. She pulled the phone away from her ear and looked at it with an attitude, like it had offended her, and then gently put it back on the hook. She then stood up from the toilet and flushed it. She washed her hands to make things more real and walked out to face Danny once again.

When Tomeka made it back to the living room, Danny was laid back on the couch, stroking his manhood. Tomeka could understand clearly why women threw themselves at him. He was fine as fuck and his dick was perfect in length and width. It was just a shame that it wasn't even worth the time one put into it. Instead of dwelling on it, Tomeka dropped her crutches to the floor and crawled to him.

"About time you came out of there. Had me thinking you was in there taking a shit. What took you so long? I get this Mandingo ready, and you in there taking your time."

"I know you didn't forget that I'm having issues walking right now, did you? And it's causing me to move a little slower."

"Don't matter. You here now. So come on and lay back. Let a nigga bust them guts open."

"I love it when you talk dirty to me."

Danny moved so Tomeka could climb on the couch. Once she was in place, he pulled her pajama bottoms down and threw them to the side. He wanted to put her in a position that she couldn't get out of, so he lifted her legs and planted one on each of his shoulders. He had thought about being gentle and realized there really was no reason to. Instead, he pushed into her like a hammer hitting the head of a nail, and in less than three minutes, he came inside of her.

He wasn't worried about getting her pregnant, because a dead bitch couldn't carry a baby. He didn't think once about his DNA being left behind, because Danny felt like he was untouchable. When he was done, he pulled out and sat back while Tomeka waited for him to make his next move.

"Ohh, come on. I was on the verge of an orgasm. Danny, can you at least finish me off? Eat it or something?"

"Eat it? Bitch, I'm not putting my mouth on community pussy. Besides, your pleasure is the least of my concerns. What I do want to know, though, is why the hell did you put me out there to Jamir like that? I thought you said you knew how to keep your mouth closed."

"You have to understand, Danny, that I didn't have a choice. Jamir brought that dude Malcolm over here to confront me face-to-face. There was no way I could look him in the eyes and lie to him. What if I'd done that? He would have killed me."

"Then I guess you would have been a dead bitch 'cause that's part of what loyalty is. You ride, or you die."

"You don't have to be so cruel about it. At least pretend that you did care a little bit. Damn."

"See, that's the problem. I don't give a damn. You think that I didn't know that you were using me to get close to Jamir? Let me tell you something. You will never have him, but with me, all you had to do was keep it one hunnit, and I would have given you the world. Now you got to pay for running your dick suckers. I can't let that go."

"Come on, Danny. You would have done the same thing if your ass was on the line, and you know that's true."

"Well, guess what? It wasn't. It wasn't my life; it was yours, and you should have ate that bullet like a real bitch would have done, but no. You had to run your fuckin' mouth and ruin everything! Now you are going to pay for that."

Danny pulled out his Glock equipped with a silencer and pointed it at her. The fear she held in her eyes made his dick hard all over again. Tomeka noticed and felt like she could use that to her advantage. The only problem was that sex with Danny didn't give her a lot of time. She wondered what was taking the person she called so long to get there. Tomeka knew if she didn't do something, she would be done, so while her heart beat rapidly, she reached out and gripped Danny's manhood.

"Why don't you go ahead and let me take care of this bad boy for one last time?"

"This sounds like a plan, but this time, I want it from the back."

Tomeka obliged and got on all fours so Danny could enter her, and as soon as he came, he put the gun to the back of her head and pulled the trigger.

Chapter 20

Cassie had never seen the sexy baller before her, but she ground her hips in front of him with purpose. The stack of big faces he had set on the table beside him was hers if he enjoyed the performance she gave, so Cassie intended to put on the best show of her life. He didn't know it, but Cassie needed that money more than ever.

At one time, dancing in the strip club was just something she would do to keep her busy on those nights Denard would be out of town, but since he had dumped her, it became a way to survive. She would often work extra hours just to make ends meet. And as bad as she wanted to pawn the engagement ring Denard left her with, she couldn't bring herself to do it. For some reason, Cassie held out hope that he would come back to her one day. She wanted to make sure she kept the ring just in case.

The baller ran his smooth hands alongside Cassie's outer thighs. Toosii filled the room with his melodic voice. *'I'm on the stage right now, singing your favorite song. Look in the crowd, and you're nowhere to be found, as they sing along. I say, you look good without no makeup on—no lashes, even better when you wake up. Umm, umm, umm.'*

Cassie closed her eyes and imagined the song being sang to her. It made her think back to when Denard would bust out with a tune just to see her smile. She couldn't believe that she'd broken his heart after everything he did. He could protect hers. Cassie already knew that her life would never be the same, and she would get used to that, although it would be hard.

"This better be a real good reason for you to be calling me right now because I got a fine ass female in front of me, and you fucking up my groove."

Cassie smiled at what she heard and then sat down beside him. He didn't seem to mind that she was so close to him, and that eased her mind even more. She continued to listen in. What she heard made her heart beat even faster.

"Alright, good work, but don't let that nigga go anywhere. I'm on my way, but it's gonna take me a minute because I'm not close by. Do whatever you got to do to keep him there, and you will be rewarded greatly."

"Sorry, little mama, but I've been trying to catch up with this nigga Danny for a minute now. Muthafucka owes me, and he needs to pay up. I just can't let this opportunity pass me by. However, I'm going to leave you with this stack because you damn sure earned it. You can also trust and believe that after I handle this, I'm coming back for you, so make sure your pretty ass is where I can find you. I promise it will be worth it."

"Of course, I'ma be here waiting. Don't take too long, though, 'cause a girl like me don't like to be kept on hold."

The baller smiled and picked up the stack of bills before handing them to Cassie. She smiled and quickly put the money in her knee-high boots before anyone else noticed. He laughed and stood to his feet so he could leave.

Cassie sat there and waited for him to walk out of the club before she jumped up and ran to the dressing room. As soon as she got there, she went to her station and grabbed her cell phone. Something in her gut told her that he had been talking about the same Danny she had messed with, the one she lost her whole relationship behind. But she couldn't fully blame him, because it took two to tango.

Cassie pressed the numbers on the phone so fast, she swore she had dialed the wrong number, and she almost hung up until she heard Danny's voice come from the other side. Hearing him brought back memories of the good time they shared, and it made her realize that she was doing the right thing.

"Danny, where are you at? Wherever it is, you need to leave now."

"Hold up. Who in the hell is this?"

"For real, Danny? You don't even know my damn voice? You got that many other bitches calling your phone?"

"Come on, Cassie. I'm just messing with you. I could never forget your voice, so chill the fuck out. Why are you calling me, though? I gave Denard my word that I wouldn't communicate with you, so what's going on?"

"Look. I know what you promised, but could you please come scoop me up?"

"Now, you see, that's pushing it. You and I both know what happens when we're around each other, so that might not be a good idea."

"Damn it, Danny, listen to me. I was just dancing for this nigga who got a phone call from someone about your location. That muthafucka cut his session short so he can go to wherever you are. He told whoever it was to hold you until he showed up, so I'm just calling you, trying to save your got damn life. You are in danger right now, and you need to leave from there."

Danny already knew who Cassie was talking about, but he was amazed by the way she looked out for him and his well-being. He thought she would have been bitter about the way everything happened between them, but instead, she still had his back. Because of that, he couldn't leave her hanging. Danny knew that a man's word would go long way, but he was about to break his, and he dared a muthafucka to check him about it.

"A'ight, but be ready. I'm on my way, Cassie, baby."

Once the call disconnected, Cassie held the phone close to her heart. She felt good about the call she had just made because she wouldn't have been able to sleep at night if something had happened to Danny, especially something she could have prevented. She didn't care what anyone thought, not even Denard.

Cassie wasn't sure how far away Danny was, but she wanted to be ready when he got there. She got all her things because she had no plans of ever going back there. She wasn't sure what she would do, but she knew she had to leave dancing behind, hopefully. Then he wouldn't make her regret it.

When Cassie stepped out into the parking lot, she cursed herself for not having a jacket. The cool breeze gave her chills, but what eased her mind was the thought of being warm next to Danny. Cassie wasn't sure what he would say if he inquired about who the man was. She'd been so caught up in that stack of bills that she had failed to ask him his name.

Cassie quickly thought back to the good girl she used to be. She knew that her father had to be turning over in his grave because he had expected so much more from her growing up. Cassie was never boy crazy. Now she was bucking on her man and shaking her ass for strangers. She hated to admit it, but she had turned out just like her mother, something she swore she would never do.

Cassie would forever regret what she had done to Denard, but there wasn't shit she could do to change it. She figured that she might as well live her life and stop dwelling on what could have been. The mistake she made would never be forgotten, but Cassie knew she had to move on.

No sooner than she pushed Denard out of her mind, Danny pulled up. Cassie couldn't figure out what it was about him that made her so wet, but he definitely had her drenched. She couldn't wait to have him inside of her again.

"Hey, you just gonna stand there and daydream about another nigga, or you gonna get your ass in?"

Danny's voice broke Cassie from her trance she had fallen into and caused her to smile. She opened the passenger door and got in his ride without a care in the world. Deep in her heart, Danny wasn't truly who she wanted, but he was her second choice and would just have to do. Cassie decided that she would be ok with that for as long as she had to be.

"Don't be rushing me when you took forever to get here. I was out here freezing my ass off."

"Yeah, well, what are you complaining about? You already know I got something to warm you up real quick—if you're ok with it."

"Yeah, well, are you sure? Because I don't want to be the reason you break some kind of code."

"Too late for that. It's already been broken, so I might as well make it worth it. Besides, you should have told me that Denard was your man from the jump. Then I could have handled things a little differently."

"Well, now you know, even though it's a little late. I really just want to move on and forget about what happened. It's done and over with, and we can start fresh if you want to. I can be all yours now."

"Not if that nigga that's looking for me can help it. His dick probably gets hard from thoughts of killing me."

"So, you know who it is? Because I did forget to ask him his name. I guess I was too caught up in the moment."

"Yeah, I do know who it is, and it's all good, though. This muthafucka pressed up about a dyke bitch that deserved to die. To get me, though, he gonna have to get up real early. You know what I'm saying?"

"I hope you're right, Danny, because I would hate to see anything happening here, but I do have to ask. Do you think he has something to do with what happened to your kids and their mutha?"

Danny went silent and thought about what she had just asked him. Thinking back on the situation brought back memories of Raleigh and emotions he held inside. Danny still found it hard to believe that they were gone, but he knew it was karma for all that he'd done. Some of the things were unforgivable, and he knew that, one day, it would all come back to him because no sin shall go unpunished.

"You know, Cassie? What happened to them was uncalled for, but it was really meant for me, and he had everything to do with it. My life has been spared so many times, and I don't even know why. I'm not gonna lie. This shit is harder on me, knowing that I'll never see my seeds bloom, but a nigga sure is happy to be alive."

Cassie nodded her head as if she agreed with him, but deep inside, she wished it had been him. Then maybe she would still have Denard in her life. She knew that she was wrong to feel that way, but she just couldn't help herself. Denard had been her one true love, and Cassie knew that no other man would ever love her the way that he did. However, since she messed up and lost, she had to settle for what she could.

"I'm happy that you're alive too, Danny."

"You sure about that? I mean, I'm partly the reason you ain't with your man right now."

"And yet here I am, sitting beside you. Funny how that worked out, huh? Must have been meant to be."

"Guess we'll see, won't we?"

"Yeah, Danny, I guess we will."

"You already know what's going to happen if Denard finds out that we messing around again, don't you? Are you prepared for that?"

"Well, it's really no longer Denard's business what I do or who I do it with. He was the one who let me go instead of forgiving me and letting me have another chance. So that's his loss, right?"

"Yeah, but the real question is, what if he would have pushed that shit away and took you back? Would you still be here with me?"

Cassie found it hard to answer the question, so she didn't. She loved Denard with all she had but also enjoyed messing around with Danny. The excitement Danny brought to her life kept her on her toes, so she had to be completely honest with herself. She would much rather have Denard. Yeah, at times, he could be boring, but he always was a safe bet.

When Cassie was with Denard, she was treated with love and respect, and her needs were more important than his. Cassie knew that if she had told him how lonely she had been, he would have changed his whole routine. Cassie didn't want to be selfish, though, so she let him do his thing while she did hers, and for a minute, it seemed to work out just fine.

As soon as Danny pulled up to their favorite hotel, all thoughts of Denard were pushed to the back of her mind. However, Cassie wondered if she was making the right decision. She knew there was only one way to find out, so before she stepped out of the car, she had one question she needed Danny to answer. His response would help her determine her future.

"So, I guess this means I won't have to dance at the club anymore?"

"And what makes you think that? Shaking that ass puts that money in your bank, right? How else you gonna survive?"

At that point, Cassie knew she had made the wrong choice, but she also knew it was too late. Instead of complaining, though, she decided to use it to her advantage. Danny wanted to know how she would survive without dancing, and she would show him because, last time she checked, he had a bounty over his head. Cassie was going to cash in on it. Karma was a muthafucka, but she damn sure paid well.

Chapter 21

Jamir pulled into the parking lot of Tomeka's building as Denard followed closely behind. He found it strange that Blount had just pulled out from there as well. Last he heard, Blount couldn't stand Tomeka, so none of it made sense. He had Jamir's information on what had really happened with Raw, but he had no reason to show up there again unless Tomeka had more to say.

Jamir parked his ride and quickly got out. He didn't bother to wait for Denard. He had a feeling in his gut about what he would find when he entered Tomeka's apartment. He knew without a shadow of a doubt that Danny had gone there just to confront her, but once Jamir stepped into the apartment, he only saw one body. That meant Danny had been long gone before Blount even showed up.

At first, Jamir thought Tomeka may have been used as a shield, but once he saw the position her naked body had been left in, it told a different story. Tomeka had been shot in the back of the head after a moment of pleasure. She didn't even see the bullet coming.

Jamir knew that Danny could be ruthless. He wondered if he could really be that cold to do her like this. He didn't want to speculate, so he didn't even try. Just as Jamir pulled out his cell phone to call the cleanup crew, Denard walked up behind him.

"Damn, who the hell did she piss off? That shit looks crazy."

"Yeah, they did her real dirty. I'm about to call the crew, get them over here to clean this mess up."

"So you're cleaning up the next man's mess? Shit, you should turn your ass around and get up out of here, as far away as possible. This ain't your problem."

"Now, it may not be mine, but I can't be sure if it's not Danny's. I know he was here. I can feel it all in my gut, but I can't be certain that he was. I gotta take care of it just in case."

"That's real, but would that nigga do the same thing for you? And what if it wasn't him? You sure she's the only one he did like that?"

Jamir looked at Denard with concern in his eyes and then walked away. He pulled his weapon and went from room to room just to make sure that no one else had been left slumped over. Once he saw that it was all clear, he breathed a sigh of relief and placed his gun back into the waist of his jeans. Jamir then walked back into the living room where he'd left Denard and pulled out his phone once again. He placed the call to the cleanup crew and hung up. Jamir took one more look at Tomeka and shook his head. He couldn't believe that she had been left like that.

"Come on, Denard. The cleanup boys will be pulling up soon, and we need to be gone before they get here."

"Why we gotta be gone if they work for you? Shouldn't we stay to make sure the job gets done?"

"They don't even know they work for me."

"Ok, I get it, but what about Danny's ass? How the hell are we going to find him? Because it seems like he done went into hiding. Shouldn't we be coming up with a plan?"

"You sure tryin' find him real bad. Y'all cool, right?"

"Cool. Just trying to look out and help him catch that muthafucka that took my cousin's life. I ain't got no beef or anything like that, though, if that's what you wanted to know."

"Just saying, bro. I mean I know how you felt and still feel about your girl, and I also know that you ain't over it. I'm with you. That nigga was dead ass wrong. And the only thing savin' him is that he really don't know that she belongs to you. Now that he does, I'm sure he'll respect that."

"You sure got a lot of confidence in your boy. He never tried to fuck one of your bitches, huh?"

"Well, since I don't have any bitches for him to fuck, the answer is no. I be hearing shit all the time, but I ain't ask the nigga, so until it's proven, I have to say that he's kept it a hundred with me."

"Yeah. What about your little sis? You was ok with him sticking dick to Missy? I thought that was a code of violation."

Jamir looked at the nigga and thought about punching him just for mentioning her name. Several people had tried to tell him that Danny and Missy had messed around, but Jamir had to dismiss those rumors because they couldn't be proven. If Danny said it wasn't true, then he had no choice but to believe him.

Just as Jamir was about to comment, the headset on his cell phone rang. He checked to see who it was, and as soon as he saw the name Erica, he sent it straight to voicemail.

"Come on. Let's get up out of here. Or you want to stick around and be a witness to something that you ain't got shit to do with?"

"I don't know. I know the old saying: never leave a witness behind."

The two of them walked out of the apartment and went back to their rides. As soon as Jamir got in his, he felt his cell phone buzzing again. He knew that it was probably Erica trying to call back, so he ignored it. He just didn't have the time for her bullshit today. Shit just wasn't adding up. Jamir had grown tired of muthafuckas telling him about Missy and her secrets. He just wanted to know the truth.

As Jamir led Denard down the backstreets, the fiends stood by and watched and waved. However, he wasn't on a money-making mission at that time, so they would have to wait. He finally pulled in behind Old Man Nat's and killed his entire engine. Not even a minute later, Denard pulled in beside him.

Together, the two of them would sit, wait, and hope that Danny would show his face. After a couple of hours, they gave up and decided to call it a night.

"Come on. A nigga is good and tired. I have to catch up with you later."

"Alright, that's straight. I think I'm gonna go ahead and take it in too. I'll holler if I see him."

The two of them bumped fists, and then Denard got into his truck and drove away. Jamir let out a sigh and started his ride, but before he could put it in gear, his cell phone buzzed again. When he saw that Erica had put in nine-one-one, he answered, just in case it was about his daughter.

"Damn, Erica, why the hell are you blowing up my line? This better be real important."

"Jamir, you need to come get me. I got a lot to say, and I promise you're gonna want to listen."

Jamir got Erica's location to pick her up. He hoped she wasn't just trying to get close to him, because he wouldn't. Little did he know, he needed to hear exactly what she had to say.

Chapter 22

Dany knocked on the door like he was an officer of the law, still pissed because Cassie dissed him when he told her that she wouldn't keep dancing at the club. She had life messed up if she thought he was going to take care of her and pay her bills. She should have thought about that before she cheated on Denard because Danny wasn't in the business of providing for hoes. They wanted to mess with him, then he was their man, but other than that, they could kiss his ass.

"What's up? God damn, it's good to see you. It's only been like forever since your black ass stopped by. Come on in and tell me the word."

Drake opened the door with a smile on his face and greeted Danny with a brotherly hug. It had been a while since Danny had visited his cousin, so it was long overdue. Not many people even knew that the two of them were family, and that was how they wanted it. They felt like things were safer that way, and so far, both of them had managed to keep breathing.

Drake was eight years older than Danny and much deeper in the in the game. However, Drake wasn't into pushing dope. His forte was running guns. Drake was the man to see. He had customers calling on him from all over the state, and every one of them respected his flow. Drake never cheated anyone, which gained him mad respect, but he had weaknesses.

Drake messed with every female there was. They threw pussy at him, and his babies by several different women proved it. He never cared whose bitch it was; he just wanted to fuck.

"Good to see you, cuz. I was in the neighborhood, so I decided to stop by and catch up on things. You cool with that?"

"Hell yeah. You know you always welcome at my place, and you know I still got a position for you on my team if you ever want it."

"I know, and I appreciate it, but we don't need no muthafucka to start figuring shit out. Besides, I think it works out better with each of us running our own side. You know what I'm saying?"

"I understand, and I can't do nothing but respect it. Anyway, you've been out here on the block?"

"Nah, I was about to get up and get in some pussy, but that bitch tripped out on me. Something in her head told her that I was going to wife her and pay her bills while she sat on her ass at home. The fuck she was thinking? I had to tell that hoe to get the hell on."

"Damn, playa. You ruthless as hell with them. But I feel where you're coming from. I heard about Trish, and I'm sorry. You found out who pulled the plug on that yet?"

"Yeah, the streets have been talking, and I'm certain they know what they're talking about."

"Let me in on it. You know I keep them bangers, and I don't mind taking them muthafucka out."

"You good, cuz, and I know you got my back, but this is my battle, and I'd hate myself if you got involved if something goes wrong. I need you to keep breathing, Drake. Even if I'm not."

"Appreciate the love, but you know I'd eat a hollow point for you.

"Thanks, cuz, but you never have to worry about being put in a position to do that."

"So, tell me. You still pushing for that nigga, Jamir?"

"Something like that, but I'm trying to branch out and do my own thing. A nigga might be the boss now, but soon, I'm taking over everything. His ass gonna have to pull over and get in the back seat. He just don't know. Shit, you're the only muthafucka I got loyalty to. Everyone else can suck my dick."

The two cousins shared a laugh, and then Drake pulled out a blunt. He wanted to show Danny some love while he was there because he never knew when he would see him again. Drake lit the blunt and inhaled it before he passed it off to Danny. Then, out of nowhere, a thought came to Drake's mind.

"Hey, cuz, did your boy ever find out you were fucking his little sister?"

"Hell no. Muthafucka questioned shit at times, but you know I straight denied it. I had to get rid of that bitch, though, because she was about to blow up my spot. Called herself catching feelings and shit. Bro, I had put that hoe on that pipe, and after that, I knew she was done. I had a bad batch cooked up, and the rest was history. Jamir never knew I had a hand in her death, and I plan on keeping it that way. I do miss that good pussy, though."

Danny pulled on the blunt real hard and then passed it back. He liked smoking on that green, but he really preferred it iced up with some white. He never told his cousin that, though, because he knew what he would think about him, so Danny just enjoyed the bare blunt as it was.

"Hey, cuzzo, you're more than welcome to chill for as long as you need to, but I'm about to go back to bed. I got a fine ass bitch back there waiting on me, and I'm ready to give her that pussy makeover. I'm gonna have her crying for Jesus to save her."

"Nigga, you shot the fuck out, but it's all good. I can't do nothing but respect your gangster. Shit, at least one of us can get some pussy tonight. Looks like I'm gonna have to sale a bitch dream to get me some."

"Hey, you got to do what you got to do. It ain't the time to waste if it works."

Drake passed the rest of the blunt back to Danny and walked away without taking another pull. Danny set it in the ashtray and leaned back in the recliner. He was just about to close his eyes and take a quick nap when he felt his cell phone buzzing. When he saw that it was Cassie, he almost sent it to voicemail, but he chose to answer it instead.

"I hope you're calling me with a different mindset because I don't have time to play these games with you."

"Actually, I'm calling you to apologize. I know that I was wrong, Danny. I mean, I know you just suffered a terrible loss, and I shouldn't have expected so much from you so soon. Maybe I could have another chance?"

"A'ight, tell me where you at, and I'll come scoop you up."

After Cassie told Danny where she was, he hung up. For some reason, the call had given him an uneasy feeling. Cassie sounded like she had rehearsed the lines she spoke over and over. It was as if someone else had guided her on what to say. She had Danny messed up if she thought he was going to fall by her bullshit.

Danny saw Drake's keys on the counter and decided to switch rides. He texted him, although he was in the next room, and told him that he would return with his ride. Then Danny left his own keys and took Drake's. Cassie's fate would depend on what he pulled up on. For her sake, she had better hope it was nothing.

Chapter 23

Jamir slowly pulled up in front of the laundromat where Erica told him she would be. He instantly became irritated because she was nowhere in sight. Jamir quickly grabbed his phone so he could give her a call and curse her out for wasting his time, but before he had a chance to press a number, she happened to appear from around the corner. He wondered where she had been all night because she looked rough. Jamir hoped that nothing had happened to his daughter, and as soon as Erica got in his ride, he questioned her.

"The hell is up with you blowing up my number like that? Something going on with my daughter?"

"You know, Jamir? It's so funny how you seem so concerned about it. I mean, for a father who hardly ever stops by to check on his daughter, it's actually a little strange. If you wasn't so damn busy in the streets, you would know that she is fine."

"Don't get fuckin' smart, Erica, because now is not the time. Just tell me what was so important that you had to call me out here."

"I called you because I had to warn you. Now, you're not gonna like it."

"Erica, can you just get on with it? I got shit I need to handle, and you holding me up."

"Ok, damn. You are so impatient. Anyway, I've been chilling with this nigga called Drake. You know, the one who pushes them all the guns? Well, we're in the bedroom, getting one in, and a knock comes at his front door. I didn't want him to get up off me because, oh man, that dick was getting good and—"

"Ok, Erica, I know you've been getting dicked down, and I don't give a damn. What you do with your pussy is your business. I just need you to get to the point."

"Anyway, like I said, a knock came at the front door, and guess who it was? You're no-good-ass friend Danny, who just happens to be Drake's cousin, and he had a mouthful to say. He had no clue that I was there because I stayed in the bedroom. However, you know my nosy ass made sure the room door hadn't been closed. I needed to be able to listen, and you are going to be glad that I did. I took it upon myself to record it, every word that Danny said, and once you hear it, you ain't going to ever look at him the same."

Erica pulled out her cell phone, and before she passed it to Jamir, she made sure to enter her password and open it. She hoped that the gesture would give her some brownie points. She tried to find everything she could think of to get Jamir to mess with her again, but nothing seemed to work. Erica had run out of options, but the conversation she had stumbled upon had to put her back in Jamir's good graces.

Erica stayed quiet while Jamir listened to the whole voicemail. The man was supposed to have his back, and even though he never fully trusted Danny, he still looked at him as if he were family. The conversation didn't get too interesting to him at first. Jamir had always known that Danny wanted to be in his spot, but he also knew that it would never happen.

Danny wasn't strong enough to run a street crew. Hell, he could barely keep up with the one corner he had. Plus, he messed around with all of his profit, and no one truly respected him. Yeah, Danny got plenty of pussy, but he could never hold a bitch down. He was too selfish for that.

Jamir had given him many opportunities to pull himself up, but Danny could never hold on. Jamir continued to listen to Danny talk, and Erica said it was his cousin. Jamir had heard of Drake, but he had never messed with him on the weapons side. He never needed his guns, because as far as he knew, there was no beef for him to cook up. The gun that Malcolm had gifted him was enough, and he hoped it would stay that way.

Jamir was getting bored and was about to pass Erica's phone back to her when he heard Missy's name. His heart felt as if it would jump out of his chest when Danny admitted to messing around with her. Jamir had always thought that the two of them were close, but to find out it was more than he imagined cut him deeply.

Jamir began to breathe heavily when he heard it was Danny who got his sister hooked on drugs. She had denied it, but Jamir knew the signs. He gave her the benefit of the doubt because he wanted to believe she would never lie to him. What really took Jamir's breath away was hearing it was Danny, his right hand, that had caused Missy's death.

Jamir turned and looked at Erica with tears forming in his eyes. He didn't want to believe what he'd heard, so he played it over again to make sure he heard it right. Each time he played it, he became even more angry, and if Danny had been standing in front of him, he would have put a bullet right in his head.

"Jamir. You wanna give me my phone back now? I think you've heard enough."

"No, I'm gonna need to keep it for a little while. I need to make sure this nigga knows why he has a gun between his eyes."

"So what the hell am I supposed to do? What if someone tries to get a hold of me? I need to be able to answer my phone."

"I'm sure you'll be ok if you miss a dick or two. You done probably already had enough to last you a whole lifetime anyway. I'm gonna need the password though so I can open this back up."

"Hell no. I'm not about to give you access to all of my business. Some things just ain't for you to know, so you gonna have to let me ride for this one. I'll open it back up when you need it."

"No. What you gonna do is take your ass home and tend to our daughter. I'm not about to let you get put in a position to lose your life. One of us needs to be here for her just in case shit don't go as planned. Now, give me the password so I can go handle this."

"Well, at least it's good to know that you give a damn."

"You should have thought about that before you brought me this. Missy was my family, and I have to avenge what happened to her. If I lose my life in the process, then so be it. Now, I'm gonna tell you one more time—give me the muthafuckin' password."

The thought of Jamir getting killed made Erica cry, but she understood where he was coming from and hoped it wouldn't turn out badly for him. She knew, once he heard the recording, he would go after Danny. She didn't want to keep it from him. He had been trying out on the streets to find who was responsible for Missy's downfall, which led to her death, but no one would talk. If he ended up losing his life, she would feel responsible. What would she tell her daughter?

"Jamir, I brought you this because I know you have been wondering. I just wanted you to have peace with it. At least now you know Danny can't be trusted."

"Bitch, I ain't never trusted Danny. I've always had a feeling in my gut that he was a shady nigga, and tonight, you proved my feeling to be right. And if you thought letting me listen to this would bring me some peace about Missy, then you don't know me very well. I won't have peace until this nigga is six feet under. And like I said before, I don't care if I have to lose my life to avenge my sister. Now, if you care anything about me and my well-being, you'll give me what I asked you for so I can go handle this."

Erica hesitated again but ended up giving Jamir the password, and then he drove her to her apartment. When she got out of the car, he was about to leave but knew that he needed to go inside and see his only child. Jamir hadn't been the type of father she deserved, and although he knew he should do better, he wasn't sure he had it in him.

Jamir walked into the apartment behind Erica, and while she paid the young girl who babysat their daughter, he continued to his little angel's room. When he got there, she was in her crib asleep, like she didn't have a care in the world, and he hoped it would always be that way. He stood and stared down at her for a while. Then he turned around and walked out. He hoped that he would be around to see her graduate from college one day, but he wasn't sure how his cards had been shuffled. Jamir could only pray he would be dealt a good hand.

"Yo, Erica? Make sure you take good care of her and let her know every day how much I loved her. Can you do that for me?"

"Jamir, stop talking like that, ok?"

"Look, just take care of her. I gotta get outta here."

Jamir stopped in front of Erica and gave her a kiss on the forehead, a gesture he could not explain, but one he felt warranted. He felt her inhale deeply and close her eyes. He knew it was because she couldn't stand to see him walk away, not knowing if she would ever see him again. Once he got back inside his ride, the first thing Jamir did was call Denard to let him know what was up. Shit in his life finally came to a head, and he needed someone to know where he was headed so they could back him up if needed. It wasn't that Jamir was scared; he just wanted to be cautious. After he hung up with Denard, he took a minute to himself, and then he made his next call.

Chapter 24

Danny drove Drake's Mercedes truck like he had been driving it all his life. He liked the fact no one would know it was him who was behind the wheel. If someone had some smoke, it would give him the advantage.

When he pulled into the parking lot of the hotel, he cruised around it a couple of times without stopping. Once he felt like things were safe, he parked, but still, Danny wouldn't get out. Instead, he leaned the seat back and pulled out his phone to call Cassie. She answered on the first ring.

"Damn, Danny, where the hell are you? I'm up here with nothing on, having to play with her myself, and I need you like right now."

"Well, right now will have to be later. Put your clothes back on and come outside. I got somewhere special I wanna take you."

"Uh, well, ok. Just give me a couple of minutes, and I'll be ready. Where are you at?"

"Do what I said and meet me at the sign in the front of the office, and don't be long."

He hung up on her and waited for a few minutes to pass, and then he saw as Cassie walked out to the front. He watched her as she went to the spot he told her to be, and then he looked around the parking lot to make sure no one followed her.

Once he felt like he was in the clear, he started the truck up and drove to the front of the hotel where Cassie stood.

When he pulled up, she backed away from the vehicle like she was being tried, but once Danny rolled down the window, she smiled and got in.

"Baby, this is a nice ass ride. I didn't expect to be picked up like this."

"You like it, huh? Well, don't get used to it because I'm just borrowing it. However, if things go as planned, I might just be able to own one."

"Ohh, I like the sound of that. Just don't forget about me when you need someone to keep the sheets warm."

Danny was just about to respond when he felt his phone vibrate. He started to ignore it but decided against it. He thought it was probably Drake checking on his ride, so without looking at the number, Danny answered it.

"Damn, nigga, I ain't been gone that long in this baby. I'll return it in a little while. Besides, it impressed my little lady, and you know a nigga working on getting that pussy."

"D, don't know who you think you're talking to, but what the hell are you talking about?"

"Oh, damn. What's up, Mir? My bad, bro, I thought you was my boy calling about his ride. What's up though?"

"What's up is I came up on something big, and you need to know. I can't leave you behind. Why don't you meet me at the park so we can handle this? That is, unless you're done making the big boy moves."

"Hell no. A nigga like me ain't gonna never stop moving. You know you can always count on me to make things happen. Give me a few minutes, though, because I'm on the other side of town."

"Ok, I'll be waiting for you."

Danny smiled at the thought of another come-up. And if it was as big as Jamir predicted, it would be just what he needed to obtain his spot. He turned his head and looked at Cassie with a smile. He didn't want to waste any time by turning around and taking her back, so she would have to join on him on the ride. Danny didn't think her Jamir would mind. If he did, he would no longer follow Jamir's rules. Instead, it'd be the ones he had made for himself.

Danny told himself that he would push the product right to fill his bank account. He had grown tired of lagging behind other people when he knew he had the potential to get ahead. He thought of a few niggas he would pull to form his street crew. And unlike Jamir, niggas would only get one chance with him. Then, he wouldn't mind taking a life. Only his meant something to him anyway.

"What are you over there thinking about so hard, and where are we going?"

Cassie's voice broke Danny's train of thought. He needed a loyal bitch to ride beside him on his journey, and it damn sure wasn't going to be her. She had messed up by cheating on Denard, and Danny felt like she would do the same to him. So that night would be her last; she just didn't know it. However, until he could rid himself of her, he had to play the role to get to the end.

"Ohh, baby, I'm just over here thinking about how we about to come up. You ready to step into the role of a boss chick? Because I'm about to soar to the top. You down or what?"

"Whatever, Danny. To me, you've always been at the top, but if you want to go higher, I'm with you all the way. Make sure you always remember that."

"Ok, then sit back and enjoy this ride because it's going to be a smooth one from here on out."

Danny felt Cassie was full of shit and she would do him just like she did Denard. The malice in her voice was loud and clear, but she would have to get up a little earlier in the morning to pull one over on him. Cassie was deadweight to him, and he didn't need anything to hold him back. He would fuck her one more good time and then throw her in the bitch. She would no longer be needed.

When he came up, all of what Danny would do was at the forefront of his mind—the money, cars, and the hoes would be within his reach because he would take his rightful spot. True enough, he could have risen long before, but he had been so irresponsible with his loot. Those days were behind him, though. He swore to himself he would not make those same mistakes.

When Danny finally made it to the park, he pulled in with caution. It wasn't that he didn't trust Jamir, but someone else could have been waiting in the darkness. Danny was certain he had plenty of enemies, and most of them smiled in his face. That was just the way things went in the streets, and it would never change.

"Ok, you just sit on back and watch your man work, and if you see anything out of the ordinary, buzz my line. You got me?"

"Ohh, of course I got you. I'ma always have you, Danny. That much, you can believe."

Danny turned off his ride and was about to get out. At first, he was going to leave the keys in the ignition, but he thought better of that. What if Cassie got spooked and left him hanging? He couldn't chance that, so he took the keys with him and left her alone.

Cassie shook her head in disbelief because if he thought she was just going to sit back, he was sadly mistaken. Cassie was no dumb bitch, and she knew how the game ended, so before she allowed another minute to pass, she pulled out her phone and made the call that she'd been waiting to make all night—one that would alter Danny's life forever.

Chapter 25

Jamir felt relieved when Danny finally showed up because at first, he didn't believe he would. However, Danny was a greedy ass nigga, and if any opportunity came, he would jump right on it. Jamir could also tell that someone had come along with him, and since he didn't know who it was, he got his nine ready. He also had Denard a short distance away just in case.

"Damn, D, it's about time you got here. I was just about to give up and go home and find somebody else who was serious about getting this paper. What took you so long, and who you brought with you?"

"Man, I told you I was across town. I had to pick Cassie up right before you called me, and instead of wasting time and taking her back, I brought her with me."

"You mean the same Cassie that fucked with Denard? Nigga, you is crazy."

"Look, she single now, so she don't belong to anybody, and you know I'm not about to let some pussy go to waste. That nigga should have done his job and kept a leash on that bitch, and she'd be in his bed right now instead of in my passenger seat. It wasn't my fault he couldn't put it down like a real G. She just knows what's good for her."

"Boy, you crazy as hell. He's gonna be pissed when he find this out."

"The hell are you so worried about how Denard feels? When you muthafuckas became tight? Because last time I checked, I was your boy, not him."

"Nah, bro. I'm just saying you gave that man your word, and in the streets, that means something."

"How about, *fuck Denard and the code of the streets*? Let's handle what we here for."

"A'ight. Let's handle it, but before we do, I just got something I need you to listen to, just something I happened to stumble upon. I'm sure you're going to want to hear it too."

Jamir didn't even give Danny a chance to respond before he pushed play on the recording. He watched as Danny's eyes grew big in disbelief. The one thing Jamir had searched for had been in front of him all along. He just didn't want to believe it. A nigga he had known almost all his life had betrayed not only him but the ones he loved. That was unforgivable, and tonight, he had to pay for that.

"Look, Jamir, I can explain. Missy came up to me. I know you knew she had a crush on me. Shit, she was a pretty ass bitch. Any nigga would have loved to get up in that. It just happened to be me she wanted. You can't be mad at me. The one you should be mad at is your old man, cracked-out genes. I can't help it that Missy followed in his footsteps. You know what I'm saying?

"Are you fucking serious right now? I looked at you like family, you funky muthafucka! You knew what my family went through because of my pops, and you still turned my sister on to that shit! She is gone, Danny, and ain't never coming back, and it's all because of you! Every day, you rode beside me. Nigga, you smiled up in my face like shit smelled good, and the whole time, you were such snake behind my back! But you gonna have to pay for that. I can't let this shit get pushed to the side for another second. This has got to be handled. I was supposed to be able to trust you around my people, but you let me down. That's some foul ass shit."

Jamir drew his weapon and caused Danny to flinch because he had somehow forgotten to bring his. Danny had been so focused on the thought of taking Jamir's spot, everything else had been pushed to the side, even his protection. Danny hoped that Cassie would see what was going on and be smart enough to grab his gun from under the seat and at least try to defend him. Little did he know, Cassie had her own issues going on.

Denard had seen it was Cassie in the ride with the nigga who had given his word. His heart was broken once again because Denard had been seriously thinking about taking her back. He couldn't believe she had run back to Danny so quickly, but he was going to make sure it didn't happen again.

While Jamir handled his business with Danny, Denard decided to handle his with the woman he was supposed to spend his life with. The one thing he thought he would never do was the thing he now *had* to do. He crept up to the truck slowly. Luckily, the driver side door had been left unlocked, and it gave Denard easy access. By the time Cassie realized the door had been opened, Denard was already inside.

Before she had a chance to scream, he sent her back to her maker. Denard didn't even give her a chance to explain, because honestly, wasn't shit he wanted to hear. Once he pulled the trigger and claimed her last breath, he reached over and pulled the engagement ring he'd given her off her finger. Where she was going, she wouldn't need it anyway.

Denard sat and stared at the ring and wondered what could have been. He'd been so focused on what he had done that he didn't realize he had company until it was too late. The bullet penetrated his skull with vengeance. He didn't even get a chance to look his killer in the eyes before *his* were shut forever, and the silencer kept the shot from being heard. Danny and Jamir had no clue that they had no backup and continued on.

"Come on, Mir. We can work this shit out. It ain't gotta be like this."

"What you mean, work this out? Nigga, working this out won't bring Missy back, so you can kiss my ass. She ain't deserve to die like that, but you? You a different story. Everyone tried to tell me that you was snaking my ass, but I ain't listen. I wanted to believe that we was keeping shit real with each other, but I was wrong. Ain't no way I can let you live, especially knowing I can't even trust you."

"Jamir, we've been partners a long time, but you was always rising, while I sank. That shit got old real quick. You always claimed we was equal, but the scales tipped on your side. How is a nigga supposed to trust that? You was always out for *self*! You ain't care about me."

"Fuck is you talking about? I always looked out! You chose to fuck off with what I gave you, while I handled mine the right way. You could have been where I am, but it wasn't really what you wanted. It's also something you couldn't have handled. You ain't got the sense to be a leader, so you would have eventually sunk yourself. Right now, I'm gonna do you a favor and take you out of your misery. You don't deserve to breathe, so I'm gonna make sure that you don't anymore."

Danny looked up and saw Blount with a gun pointed his way, but Jamir had no clue he was there. Danny wondered how Blount even knew where to find him. And then he thought about Cassie. The bitch had to have made the call, but it would be a wasted one. Not even thinking about the gun Jamir had pointed at his chest, Danny reached out and pulled his ex-partner to him. Before they could hit the ground, a shot rang out from the distance, one that would end an era.

Epilogue

Rachel sat at Jamir's bedside and cried. She'd been released early due to prison overcrowding, but she never expected to come home to what lay before her. She had to fight to get as far as she did. Erica had told the doctors not to allow her in. However, she found one who was sympathetic to what she wanted. The beeping machine told her that Jamir was still with her, but no one knew for how long. Blount had aimed at Danny, but he pulled Jamir into him as a shield, and the bullet hit him instead. Now Jamir had to fight for his life, and not even the doctors knew if he would make it.

"Hey. What you doing all that crying for? A nigga ain't left you yet."

Rachel heard Jamir's frank voice clearly. She prayed he would wake up, and he did. To her, that was a good sign that he knew better. It was time for him to follow his family and be with them once again, but first, he needed to know something.

"Ohh, Jamir, I thought I'd lost you forever."

"Don't get too happy, ma, because this is gonna be it for me. I need to know, though. Did Danny make it?"

"I think so. Jamir, no one knows where he is. He used you to dodge the bullet that was meant for him. So you need to get better and go give him what he should have gotten that night."

"Nah, that ain't how shit works. He gon' get his; you can mark my words. But hey, let's not worry about that right now. We don't have much longer, so let's make the best of it."

"Ok, but I don't know if I can let you go, so please hold on."

"Ain't gonna be able to, Rach, but I need you to know that I'ma be waiting on you to get to me. I'm sorry I wasn't the man you needed me to be, and I hope you can find a nigga to give you what you deserve. I love you, girl, and I'm gonna be watching you, so make me proud. I also need you to do me a favor."

"Anything for you, Jamir. Anything."

Jamir was growing weaker by the second, but before he closed his eyes for good, he gave Rachel one last set of directions.

"Make sure you *Bury Me A Boss*."

Lock Down Publications and Ca$h Presents Assisted Publishing Packages

Due to an increase in the price of services we have increased our prices. The prices below reflect the price increase as of 11/1/24.

BASIC PACKAGE $699 Editing Cover Design Formatting	UPGRADED PACKAGE $1000 Typing Editing Cover Design Formatting Upload eBooks to Amazon Upload Paperback to Amazon
ADVANCE PACKAGE $1,400 Typing Editing (line editing/content) Cover Design Formatting Copyright Registration Proofreading Upload eBooks to Amazon Upload Paperback to Amazon	LDP SUPREME PACKAGE $1,700 Typing Editing (line editing/content) Cover Design Formatting Copyright Registration Proofreading Set up Amazon Account Upload eBooks to Amazon Upload Paperback to Amazon Advertise on LDP's Amazon and Facebook Page

***
Other services available upon request.
Additional charges may apply

Lock Down Publications
P.O. Box 944
Stockbridge, GA 30281-9998
Phone: 470 303-9761
Email: lockdownpublications@gmail.com

Submission Guideline

Submit the first three chapters of your completed manuscript to ldpsubmissions@gmail.com. In the subject line add **Your Book's Title**. The manuscript must be in a Word Doc file and sent as an attachment. Document should be in Times New Roman, double spaced, and in size 12 font. Also, provide your synopsis and full contact information. If sending multiple submissions, they must each be in a separate email.

Have a story but no way to send it electronically? You can still submit to LDP/Ca$h Presents. Send in the first three chapters, written or typed, of your completed manuscript to:

LDP: Submissions Dept
P.O. Box 944
Stockbridge, GA 30281-9998

DO NOT send original manuscript. Must be a duplicate. Provide your synopsis and a cover letter containing your full contact information.

Thanks for considering LDP and Ca$h Presents.

NEW RELEASES

BLOODLINE OF A SAVAGE 1-3
THESE VICIOUS STREETS 1-3
RELENTLESS GOON 1-3
BY PRINCE A. TAUHID

THE BUTTERFLY MAFIA 1-3
BY FUMIYA PAYNE

A THUG'S STREET PRINCESS 1&2
BY MEESHA

CITY OF SMOKE 3
BY MOLOTTI

GET IT IN SLUGS 1 &2
BY B. STALL

STANDING ON HER BUSINESS 1&2
BY DG SANTANA

STEPPERS 1,2&3
THE REAL BADDIES OF CHI-RAQ
BY KING RIO

THE LANE 1&2
BY KEN-KEN SPENCE

THUG OF SPADES 1&2
LOVE IN THE TRENCHES 2
CORNER BOYS
BY COREY ROBINSON

TIL DEATH 3
BY ARYANNA

THE BIRTH OF A GANGSTER 4
BY DELMONT PLAYER

PRODUCT OF THE STREETS 1-3
BY DEMOND "MONEY" ANDERSON

NO TIME FOR ERROR
BY KEESE

MONEY HUNGRY DEMONS 1-2
BY TRANAY ADAMS

HUB CITY MENACE 1-3
BY J. WHITE

A THUGGISH PASSION 1&2
LAND OF DA HOOLIGANZ 1-4
KILLAZ ON STANDBY 1&2
BY IRA B.

FO'EVA ROLLIN 1&2
BY ASSA RAYMOND BAKER

THE LEVEL UP 1&3
BY LUXURY KING

Coming Soon from Lock Down Publications/Ca$h Presents

IF YOU CROSS ME ONCE 6
ANGEL V
By Anthony Fields

A THUGS STREET PRINCESS 3
By Meesha

CORNER BOYS 2
By Corey Robinson

THA TAKEOVER
By Keith Chandler

BETRAYAL OF A G 2
By Ray Vinci

SAVAGE FAMILY EMPIRE 1&2
SOULLESS GOON 1,2&3
THE DIRTY SIDE OF MONEY 1,2&3
By Prince

FOR MY ENEMY'S SAKE
AMBITIONS OF A SLIDER
FRESH OFF DA PORCH
By IRA B.

THE TRUCKLOAD 1-4
TIPPIN' THE SCALES 1-3
BAD BITCHES WIT GUNZ 3
PROBLEM SOLVED 2
By Christopher "Diesel" Hornezes

Available Now

RESTRAINING ORDER 1 & 2
By **CA$H & Coffee**

LOVE KNOWS NO BOUNDARIES 1-3
By **Coffee**

RAISED AS A GOON I, II, III & IV
BRED BY THE SLUMS I, II, III
BLAST FOR ME I & II
ROTTEN TO THE CORE I II III
A BRONX TALE I, II, III
DUFFLE BAG CARTEL I II III IV V VI
HEARTLESS GOON I II III IV V
A SAVAGE DOPEBOY I II
DRUG LORDS I II III
CUTTHROAT MAFIA I II
KING OF THE TRENCHES
By **Ghost**

LAY IT DOWN I & II
LAST OF A DYING BREED I II
BLOOD STAINS OF A SHOTTA I & II III
By **Jamaica**

LOYAL TO THE GAME I II III
LIFE OF SIN I, II III
By **TJ & Jelissa**

IF LOVING HIM IS WRONG…I & II
LOVE ME EVEN WHEN IT HURTS I II III
By **Jelissa**

PUSH IT TO THE LIMIT
By **Bre' Hayes**

BLOODY COMMAS I & II
SKI MASK CARTEL I, II & III
KING OF NEW YORK I II, III IV V
RISE TO POWER I II III
COKE KINGS I II III IV V
BORN HEARTLESS I II III IV
KING OF THE TRAP I II
By **T.J. Edwards**

WHEN THE STREETS CLAP BACK I & II III
THE HEART OF A SAVAGE I II III IV
MONEY MAFIA I II
LOYAL TO THE SOIL I II III
By **Jibril Williams**

A DISTINGUISHED THUG STOLE MY HEART I II & III
LOVE SHOULDN'T HURT I II III IV
RENEGADE BOYS 1-4
PAID IN KARMA 1-3
SAVAGE STORMS 1-3
AN UNFORESEEN LOVE 1-3
BABY, I'M WINTERTIME COLD 1-3
A THUG'S STREET PRINCESS 1&2
By **Meesha**

A GANGSTER'S CODE 1-3
A GANGSTER'S SYN 1-3
THE SAVAGE LIFE 1-3
CHAINED TO THE STREETS 1-3
BLOOD ON THE MONEY 1-3
A GANGSTA'S PAIN 1-3
BEAUTIFUL LIES AND UGLY TRUTHS
CHURCH IN THESE STREETS
By **J-Blunt**

CUM FOR ME 1-8
An LDP Erotica Collaboration

BLOOD OF A BOSS 1-5
SHADOWS OF THE GAME
TRAP BASTARD
By **Askari**

THE STREETS BLEED MURDER 1-3
THE HEART OF A GANGSTA 1-3
By **Jerry Jackson**

WHEN A GOOD GIRL GOES BAD
By **Adrienne**

THE COST OF LOYALTY 1-3
By **Kweli**

BRIDE OF A HUSTLA 1-3
THE FETTI GIRLS 1-3
CORRUPTED BY A GANGSTA 1-4
BLINDED BY HIS LOVE
THE PRICE YOU PAY FOR LOVE 1-3
DOPE GIRL MAGIC 1-3
By **Destiny Skai**

A KINGPIN'S AMBITION
A KINGPIN'S AMBITION II
I MURDER FOR THE DOUGH
By **Ambitious**

TRUE SAVAGE 1-7
DOPE BOY MAGIC 1-3
MIDNIGHT CARTEL 1-3
CITY OF KINGZ 1&2
NIGHTMARE ON SILENT AVE
THE PLUG OF LIL MEXICO 1&2
CLASSIC CITY
By **Chris Green**

A GANGSTER'S REVENGE 1-4
THE BOSS MAN'S DAUGHTERS 1-5
A SAVAGE LOVE 1&2
BAE BELONGS TO ME 1&2
A HUSTLER'S DECEIT 1-3
WHAT BAD BITCHES DO 1-3
SOUL OF A MONSTER 1-3
KILL ZONE
A DOPE BOY'S QUEEN 1-3
TIL DEATH 1-3
IMMA DIE BOUT MINE 1-6
DYING FOR LIKES
By **Aryanna**

A DOPEBOY'S PRAYER
By **Eddie "Wolf" Lee**

THE KING CARTEL 1-3
By **Frank Gresham**

THESE NIGGAS AIN'T LOYAL 1-3
By **Nikki Tee**

GANGSTA SHYT 1-3
By **CATO**

THE ULTIMATE BETRAYAL
By **Phoenix**

BOSS'N UP 1-3
By **Royal Nicole**

I LOVE YOU TO DEATH
By **Destiny J**

I RIDE FOR MY HITTA
I STILL RIDE FOR MY HITTA
By **Misty Holt**

LOVE & CHASIN' PAPER
By **Qay Crockett**

TO DIE IN VAIN
SINS OF A HUSTLA
By **ASAD**

BROOKLYN HUSTLAZ
By **Boogsy Morina**

BROOKLYN ON LOCK 1 & 2
By **Sonovia**

GANGSTA CITY
By **Teddy Duke**

A DRUG KING AND HIS DIAMOND 1-3
A DOPEMAN'S RICHES
HER MAN, MINE'S TOO 1&2
CASH MONEY HO'S
THE WIFEY I USED TO BE 1&2
PRETTY GIRLS DO NASTY THINGS
By **Nicole Goosby**

LIPSTICK KILLAH 1-3
CRIME OF PASSION 1-3
FRIEND OR FOE 1-3
By **Mimi**

TRAPHOUSE KING 1-3
KINGPIN KILLAZ 1-3
STREET KINGS 1&2
PAID IN BLOOD 1&2
CARTEL KILLAZ 1-3
DOPE GODS 1&2
By **Hood Rich**

THE STREETS ARE CALLING
By **Duquie Wilson**

STEADY MOBBN' 1-3
THE STREETS STAINED MY SOUL 1-3
By **Marcellus Allen**

WHO SHOT YA 1-3
SON OF A DOPE FIEND 1-4
HEAVEN GOT A GHETTO 1&2
SKI MASK MONEY 1&2
By **Renta**

GORILLAZ IN THE BAY 1-4
TEARS OF A GANGSTA 1/&2
3X KRAZY 1&2
STRAIGHT BEAST MODE 1&2
By **DE'KARI**

TRIGGADALE 1-3
MURDA WAS THE CASE 1-3
By **Elijah R. Freeman**

SLAUGHTER GANG 1-3
RUTHLESS HEART 1-3
By **Willie Slaughter**

GOD BLESS THE TRAPPERS 1-3
THESE SCANDALOUS STREETS 1-3
FEAR MY GANGSTA 1-5
THESE STREETS DON'T LOVE NOBODY 1-2
BURY ME A G 1-5
A GANGSTA'S EMPIRE 1-4
THE DOPEMAN'S BODYGAURD 1&2
THE REALEST KILLAZ 1-3
THE LAST OF THE OGS 1-3
By **Tranay Adams**

MARRIED TO A BOSS 1-3
By **Destiny Skai & Chris Green**

KINGZ OF THE GAME 1-7
CRIME BOSS 1-4
By **Playa Ray**

FUK SHYT
By **Blakk Diamond**

DON'T F#CK WITH MY HEART 1&2
By **Linnea**

ADDICTED TO THE DRAMA 1-3
IN THE ARM OF HIS BOSS
By **Jamila**

LOYALTY AIN'T PROMISED 1&2
By **Keith Williams**

YAYO 1-4
A SHOOTER'S AMBITION 1&2
BRED IN THE GAME
By **S. Allen**

TRAP GOD 1-3
RICH $AVAGE 1-3
MONEY IN THE GRAVE 1-3
CARTEL MONEY 1&2
By **Martell Troublesome Bolden**

FOREVER GANGSTA 1&2
GLOCKS ON SATIN SHEETS 1&2
By **Adrian Dulan**

TOE TAGZ 1-4
LEVELS TO THIS SHYT 1&2
IT'S JUST ME AND YOU
By **Ah'Million**

KINGPIN DREAMS 1-3
RAN OFF ON DA PLUG
By **Paper Boi Rari**

THE STREETS MADE ME 1-3
By **Larry D. Wright**

CONFESSIONS OF A GANGSTA 1-4
CONFESSIONS OF A JACKBOY 1-3
CONFESSIONS OF A HITMAN
CONFESSIONS OF A DOPE BOY
By **Nicholas Lock**

I'M NOTHING WITHOUT HIS LOVE
SINS OF A THUG
TO THE THUG I LOVED BEFORE
A GANGSTA SAVED XMAS
IN A HUSTLER I TRUST
By **Monet Dragun**

QUIET MONEY 1-3
THUG LIFE 1-3
EXTENDED CLIP 1&2
A GANGSTA'S PARADISE
By **Trai'Quan**

CAUGHT UP IN THE LIFE 1-3
THE STREETS NEVER LET GO 1-3
By **Robert Baptiste**

NEW TO THE GAME 1-3
MONEY, MURDER & MEMORIES 1-3
By **Malik D. Rice**

CREAM 2-3
THE STREETS WILL TALK
By **Yolanda Moore**

THE STREETS WILL NEVER CLOSE 1-3
By **K'ajji**

LIFE OF A SAVAGE 1-4
A GANGSTA'S QUR'AN 1-4
MURDA SEASON 1-3
GANGLAND CARTEL 1-3
CHI'RAQ GANGSTAS 1-4
KILLERS ON ELM STREET 1-3
JACK BOYZ N DA BRONX 1-3
A DOPEBOY'S DREAM 1-3
JACK BOYS VS DOPE BOYS 1-3
COKE GIRLZ
COKE BOYS
SOSA GANG 1&2
BRONX SAVAGES
BODYMORE KINGPINS
BLOOD OF A GOON
By **Romell Tukes**

CONCRETE KILLA 1-3
VICIOUS LOYALTY 1-3
BLOODY MONEY BAGS
By **Kingpen**

THE ULTIMATE SACRIFICE 1-6
KHADIFI
IF YOU CROSS ME ONCE 1-3
ANGEL 1-4
IN THE BLINK OF AN EYE
By **Anthony Fields**

THE LIFE OF A HOOD STAR
By **Ca$h & Rashia Wilson**

NIGHTMARES OF A HUSTLA 1-3
BLOOD AND GAMES 1&2
By **King Dream**

GHOST MOB
By **Stilloan Robinson**

HARD AND RUTHLESS 1&2
MOB TOWN 251
THE BILLIONAIRE BENTLEYS 1-3
REAL G'S MOVE IN SILENCE
By **Von Diesel**

MOB TIES 1-7
SOUL OF A HUSTLER, HEART OF A KILLER 1-3
GORILLAZ IN THE TRENCHES
OOPS CRY TOO 1&2
THE DAUGHTER OF A CARTEL BOSS
By **SayNoMore**

BODYMORE MURDERLAND 1-3
THE BIRTH OF A GANGSTER 1-4
By **Delmont Player**

FOR THE LOVE OF A BOSS 1&2
By **C. D. Blue**

KILLA KOUNTY 1-5
TENDER
By **Khufu**

MOBBED UP 1-4
THE BRICK MAN 1-5
THE COCAINE PRINCESS 1-10
STEPPERS 1-3
SUPER GREMLIN 1-4
A GANGSTA'S SON
By **King Rio**

MONEY GAME 1&2
By **Smoove Dolla**

A GANGSTA'S KARMA 1-5
By **FLAME**

KING OF THE TRENCHES 1-3
By **GHOST & TRANAY ADAMS**

BAD BITCHES WIT GUNZ 1&2
PROBLEM SOLVED
By **"Christopher Diesel" Hornezes**

QUEEN OF THE ZOO 1&2
By **Black Migo**

GRIMEY WAYS 1-3
BETRAYAL OF A G
By **Ray Vinci**

XMAS WITH AN ATL SHOOTER
By **Ca$h & Destiny Skai**

KING KILLA 1&2
By **Vincent "Vitto" Holloway**

BETRAYAL OF A THUG 1&2
By **Fre$h**

COUNTDOWN OF A KILLA 1&2
SEX, MURDER AND GOD 1&2
GUNS DOWN, BOTTOMS UP 1&2
By Lo-Life

THE MURDER QUEENS 1-7
By **Michael Gallon**

FOR THE LOVE OF BLOOD 1-4
By **Jamel Mitchell**

HOOD CONSIGLIERE 1&2
NO TIME FOR ERROR
By **Keese**

PROTÉGÉ OF A LEGEND 1,2&3
LOVE IN THE TRENCHES 1&2
By **Corey Robinson**

THE PLUG'S RUTHLESS DAUGHTER 1&2
By **Tony Daniels**

BORN IN THE GRAVE 1-3
CRIME PAYS
By **Self Made Tay**

MOAN IN MY MOUTH
By **XTASY**

TORN BETWEEN A GANGSTER AND A GENTLEMAN
By **J-BLUNT & Miss Kim**

LOYALTY IS EVERYTHING 1-3
CITY OF SMOKE 1-3
By **Molotti**

HERE TODAY GONE TOMORROW 1&2
By **Fly Rock**

WOMEN LIE MEN LIE 1-4
FIFTY SHADES OF SNOW 1-3
STACK BEFORE YOU SPLURGE
GIRLS FALL LIKE DOMINOES
NAÏVE TO THE STREETS
By **ROY MILLIGAN**

PILLOW PRINCESS
By **S. Hawkins**

THE BUTTERFLY MAFIA 1-3
SALUTE MY SAVAGERY 1&2
By **Fumiya Payne**

THE LANE 1&2
By Ken-Ken Spence

THE PUSSY TRAP 1-5
By **Nene Capri**

DIRTY DNA
By **Blaque**

SANCTIFIED AND HORNY
by **XTASY**

BOOKS BY LDP'S CEO, CA$H

TRUST IN NO MAN
TRUST IN NO MAN 2
TRUST IN NO MAN 3
BONDED BY BLOOD
SHORTY GOT A THUG
THUGS CRY
THUGS CRY 2
THUGS CRY 3
TRUST NO BITCH
TRUST NO BITCH 2
TRUST NO BITCH 3
TIL MY CASKET DROPS
RESTRAINING ORDER
RESTRAINING ORDER 2
IN LOVE WITH A CONVICT
LIFE OF A HOOD STAR
XMAS WITH AN ATL SHOOTER

www.ingramcontent.com/pod-product-compliance
Lightning Source LLC
Chambersburg PA
CBHW071212260626
47162CB00004B/1269